Buster and the Amazing Daisy

Buster and the Amazing Daisy

Nancy Ogaz

Illustrations by Patricia Shubeck

Jessica Kingsley Publishers
London and Philadelphia

First published in the United Kingdom in 2002
by Jessica Kingsley Publishers Ltd
116 Pentonville Road
London N1 9JB, England
and
325 Chestnut Street
Philadelphia, PA 19106, USA
www.jkp.com

Copyright © Nancy Ogaz 2002
Illustrations copyright © Patricia Shubeck 2002

Second edition 2003

Library of Congress Cataloging-in-Publication Data
Ogaz, Nancy, 1955-
  Buster and the amazing Daisy / Nancy Ogaz
    p.cm.
  Summary: When Daisy, who is autistic, joins a mainstreamed class and trains Buster the rabbit for a pet show, she faces new challenges and makes new freinds.
  ISBN 1-84310-721-X (alk paper)
  [1. Autism--Fiction. 2. Mainstreaming in education--Fiction. 3. Schools--Fiction. 4. Freindship--Fiction. 5. Rabbits--Fiction. 6. Pet shows--Fiction.] I. Title.

PZ7.O3314 Bu 2002
[Fic]--dc21   2002021870
British Library Cataloguing in Publication Data
A CIP catalogue record for this book is available from the British Library

ISBN 1 84310 721 X

Printed and Bound in Great Britain by
Athenaeum Press, Gateshead, Tyne and Wear

Dedicated to my son, Devon

Contents

Chapter 1
Beware of the Bully-Pops

"Crazy Daisy is so lazy!" Marissa hissed in Daisy's ear.

Daisy scooted her desk forward, trying to escape the smell of sour milk and bananas. Ugh!

"Marissa Thornton." It was the teacher, Ms Kirby. "Would you please read the next paragraph?" She opened her eyes wide at Marissa.

"Yes, Ms Kirby." Marissa grabbed her book and peeked over Daisy's shoulder to see the page number.

You should spend less time thinking up those stupid rhymes and more time paying attention like you're supposed to, Daisy thought.

"Page fifty-four, second paragraph," Ms Kirby said.

As Marissa flipped through the book, Daisy could hear the papery flutter. She hunched her shoulders, waiting…waiting. *Crash*! The loud thump made her jump anyway. Marissa was always doing that. She didn't know how to treat a book – or a person.

"Marissa Thornton! If that book of yours drops again, you will spend the next recess returning books to their shelves. Is that understood?"

"Yes, Ms Kirby."

"Now please turn to page fifty-four and begin with the second paragraph." Everyone waited for Marissa to start reading. After a minute, Ms Kirby prompted her. "Second paragraph. 'You're never going to believe…'"

"You're never going to believe…" Marissa began. "That the leg…leg…legundory–"

"Legendary," someone whispered, helping her.

"That the legendary…uh, jack…jack…rope," Marissa stumbled over the word.

"It's 'jackalope', Marissa," Ms Kirby said.

For the next few minutes Marissa struggled to read, stopping and starting and stuttering along.

"Daisy, would you read the next paragraph?"

Daisy read. She breezed right through even the longest words.

Marissa rolled her eyes and tapped her pencil on her desk, then leaned forward to mutter in Daisy's ear. "Five! Four! Three! Two!–"

Brrrrring. The recess bell rang.

"I'll be waiting for you." Marissa gave Daisy a shark's smile and walked out the door.

Daisy jumped up and headed straight for the cage in the corner of the classroom. "Hi, Buster!" she said softly to the beautiful black bunny who lived there. He reared up on his hind legs and wiggled his nose at her. "Here you go." She poked a blueberry through the wire squares of his cage. He hopped over and gently took it from her, his whiskers tickling her fingers.

Daisy loved animals. You could probably guess this because she always wore a charm bracelet that had lots of tiny silver animals on it. But Buster was her favorite real animal. She gave him one more blueberry. "I don't know why Marissa is acting so mean. We used to walk to special resource class together – we were friends, sort of. But now – it's like she's an enemy." Daisy shook her head sadly. "It's strange, Buster. Very strange."

Daisy looked out the window and studied the playground. Marissa was nowhere in sight. Heaving a sigh of relief, Daisy cautiously slipped out of the classroom and strolled along towards the track. She gazed up at a red-tailed hawk that circled above the Christmas tree farm bordering the school.

In a nearby oak tree a pair of chickadees twittered. The October sun shone brightly, warming Daisy's shoulders. She raised her hand up so her bracelet could catch the sunlight. All the tiny animals swung and sparkled as she twisted and jiggled her wrist.

They danced beautifully. Daisy was enjoying watching them so much that she forgot to watch out for Marissa. Suddenly, she heard giggling behind her.

She turned to see several kids lined up with their hands raised and flapping.

Marissa yelled "Who're you waving at, Weirdo?" The others laughed harder.

Daisy made an X with her fingers and held them up. "If you do not cease the torture of this innocent, you shall be transformed into a stinky toad." She stomped her foot. "With warts!"

More mean laughter.

"Be gone with you, wretched toad!" Daisy shouted. "Shoo!"

"Here comes the yard monitor!" someone yelled, and Marissa and her pals scattered into the crowd on the playground.

Daisy tucked her hands into her sweatshirt pockets and hurried away. Those kids never used to tease her, but now they always seemed to follow Marissa's lead. In her mind, Daisy called them the Bully-Pops. They popped up everywhere and she knew they thought she was weird. It made her sad. And mad. If only Marissa would move to Mars!

Most of the kids at Ocean Vista were okay, although Daisy never knew quite what to say to them. When they talked, their voices were loud and fast. To Daisy, they almost sounded like a swarm of insects. *Buzzzzz.* Just listening to them wore her out sometimes. When she got too tired of the talking, she bent her head down so that her long hair hung like a silky dark curtain around her face. Worrying about Marissa wore her out too. What's she going to do to me next, Daisy wondered.

Later, at home, Daisy walked into the kitchen.

"Hi, Honey!" Her mother looked up from a sink full of soapy dishes as Daisy walked through the door. "How was school today?"

Daisy dumped her backpack on a chair. "It was okay." She headed toward the stairs. Her mother was so cheerful, sometimes it made her want to scream.

"Did you meet any nice kids today?" Mom chirped. "Make any new friends?"

"No." Daisy trudged up the stairs and into her room, banging the door closed behind her. "What are *friends* for, anyway?"

Chapter 2

Safe in the Fortress

The next day, when the recess bell rang, Daisy wished she could stay in the classroom. But it wasn't allowed. So, once again, she waited until the other kids were gone. Then she peered out the door.

Where was Marissa? Oh, over near the picnic tables. Marissa and the Bully-Pops were sitting there, eating their snacks. Daisy kept her eyes on them as she edged along the wall of the building. So far, so good… She paused. If I could just reach that crowd of kids playing ball, I could mingle. The Bully-Pops won't spot me in there. I hope.

Daisy was running towards the ball game when she heard Marissa.

"Oh, Daizeeeee! Where're you going, Daizeee? Don't you want to play with us?"

Daisy definitely did not. She raced through the middle of the ball game, dodging around the other kids. She could hear ugly laughter behind her. As she glanced over her shoulder, her hair blew across her face and, for a second, she couldn't see.

The kickball hurtled towards her. *Smack*! It struck Daisy's cheek. She tumbled down on the wet grass.

"Hey, watch where you're going!" somebody yelled.

Daisy scrambled to her feet. "Sorry!" She turned to run again, but bumped right into Marissa.

"What's the matter, Daisy? Your eyes a little hazy?" Marissa taunted.

The Bully-Pops screamed with laughter.

Daisy took a deep breath. "Stand back!" she warned. "Stand back or I'll shoot!" She poked her hand into her pocket.

"Oooh, I'm *so* scared!" Marissa pretended to cower.

"Leave me alone!" Suddenly, Daisy yanked out a rubber band and stretched it right up to Marissa's face.

Pop! The rubber band zapped Daisy's nose. She yelped and scrambled away from Marissa.

"Did you see that? What a klutz – she just shot herself in the nose!" Marissa and the other Bully-Pops fell against each other, laughing like hyenas.

Squinting, Daisy rubbed her face. I've had enough recess for today, she told herself.

Back in class, things were not much better. It was silent reading time. Every sound was magnified. Hampton Sweeney's stomach rumbled. The fan whirred. And Marissa stuck the end of her braided ponytail in her mouth and began sucking and gnawing on it. *Slurrrp, slurrrp!*

Daisy's fists clenched. She sat up straight and spoke loudly and clearly. "Actually, I think I've had enough Marissa for today."

Ms Kirby walked over to her desk. "Daisy? What's the matter?" she asked as she put her hand on Daisy's shoulder.

Daisy didn't look at her teacher. She was concentrating. Taking deep breaths, she chanted "Stay calm. Stay calm." Sometimes this worked. Sometimes it didn't.

"Daisy? Can you tell me what's wrong?" her teacher asked.

Daisy stole a quick look at Marissa. That was enough. "Aghhhh!" she screamed and stood up, almost knocking her chair over. "How can you ask what's wrong? Look!" She pointed her finger. "Look at her hair! The end is supposed to be all neat and dry! But look! It's all ragged and slimy! And that hideous slurping – it's so disgusting it makes my toes curl!"

"All right, Daisy–" Ms Kirby began.

"She's bothering me all the time! It's harassment, I tell you!"

"Okay, Daisy. Take it easy. Mrs Brawnley will be glad to have you visit her for a little while."

Daisy continued to rant and rave as Ms Kirby gently guided her out of the classroom.

"Harassment? Daisy sure likes big words," Hampton Sweeney said to no one in particular. For a few moments everyone listened to Daisy's sobs and Ms Kirby's murmurs outside the door. Then Michael Duffy dumped his water bottle over Betsy Yamato's head. Betsy yelled and a second later Ms Kirby marched back into the room.

"Boys and girls, please continue with silent reading. Marissa, you have a new desk. Up here." She tapped a desk up in the front row. "You may move your folders and things right now."

Grumbling, Marissa began to clear out her desk.

"Betsy, why is your hair – never mind, I don't want to know," Ms Kirby said.

"Where's Daisy?" Hampton asked. "Is she okay?"

"Daisy's taking a little break. She'll be fine. I want to remind you all that Daisy is new to Ocean Vista and that she deserves to be welcomed into our class." Ms Kirby looked straight at Marissa.

Someone whispered in the back of the classroom. "Do you have something to say, Michael?" Ms Kirby asked.

"It's just that…sometimes she acts kind of strange," Michael said.

"Yeah, first she acts all grown-up with these big, fancy words – then she gets upset over something silly – like Marissa's hair! It doesn't make sense," someone else remarked.

"Well, actually it does make sense when we remind ourselves that Daisy experiences the world in a very different kind of way. She may notice things that most people don't. Certain smells or sounds that most of us don't pay attention to may bother her a lot," Ms Kirby explained. She leaned back against her desk and crossed her feet. "Even her social sense is affected."

"What's social sense?" someone asked.

"Remember? We learned about it the week before Daisy joined our class. Who can explain what social sense is?" Ms Kirby walked over and scooped up the note that Michael was passing to the girl behind him. "Yes, Hampton."

"Social sense means…" Hampton began speaking. "Well, it's kind of hard to explain, but it's like the way we understand other people. Like looking at someone's face and understanding how they might be feeling."

"That's right," Ms Kirby said. "It's understanding another person's perspective or the way they think. So, even though Daisy uses these big words, she has a hard time understanding other kids."

Several children still looked puzzled. After a moment, Betsy spoke up. "Oh, yeah. I remember now. We did those activities about the senses."

Ms Kirby nodded. "Remember the one about noticing other people's expressions and the way they sit or stand or move?"

"Oh, yeah. We made different faces to show how we felt," Betsy said.

Lisa Mills waved her hand. "And we stood and walked in different ways to show different feelings – like being proud or scared or…whatever."

"That's right! Those things are part of our social sense." Ms Kirby paused. "I know it's hard to understand, but these problems with her senses make it tough for Daisy."

"But if her senses are all messed up, why does she seem so smart sometimes?" Jamie Huff wanted to know. "Like those books she reads and the way she talks – I don't get it."

"Well, first of all, her senses are not messed up – they are just different than most people's. And the reason Daisy *seems* smart is that she *is* smart." Ms Kirby shrugged her shoulders and smiled. "You know what, you guys? We're *all* different and special in our own way. We all have our talents and our problem areas." She looked around the room. "I'm confident that you will be kind to Daisy and learn to be friends with her. She needs friends just like the rest of us do."

The kids were all quiet. Someone's pencil rolled off the desk.

"Okay, let's get back to our reading." Ms Kirby sat down and watched Marissa shuffle back and forth as she moved her belongings to the new desk.

Over in Mrs Brawnley's room, it was not so quiet. Daisy stomped in, muttering furiously. "Why? Why is my life like this?"

"What's wrong, Daisy?" Cody Ramos asked, spinning his wheelchair to face her.

"Nothing! What's wrong with *you*?" she screeched.

"Sorry." Cody turned back to an alphabet game he was teaching some younger children.

"Daisy, would you like some time in the Fortress?" It was Mrs Brawnley.

"Yes, please!" Daisy shouted and scooted into the padded tent-like area. Inside, it was dim and noises were muffled. For a few minutes, she kicked and punched at the foam cushions. "Take that, Marissa! Have a pillow-sandwich!" She flung a pillow against the padded walls. Finally, she stretched out and closed her eyes. She felt all sweaty and breathless. Gradually, her breathing slowed. She peeked out.

Cody was still out there. His voice gave her the creeps – it sounded like a robot. And that tube thing was always hissing and clicking. Spooky, Daisy thought. She pulled herself back into the Fortress.

She tried to think pleasant thoughts, like Mrs Brawnley had suggested. Daisy could hear her teacher's gentle voice asking "What about riding a horse or watching dolphins leap in the waves? Just picture what would make you happy, Daisy."

Okay, I'll think of a peaceful ocean with Marissa bobbing around. And a fin, a very large shark fin, moving towards her. Daisy started humming the theme music for Jaws. Dahdum… Dahdum… Dahdum-dahdum-dahdum! She giggled. Probably not the kind of pleasant thoughts Mrs Brawnley meant. Oh, well!

Daisy peered out of the Fortress again. The little kids were gone. Cody was talking to the teacher while a lady fussed with the equipment attached to his wheelchair. Daisy crawled out of the dark and headed back to her own classroom.

Chapter 3

Friends and Fists

The next day started out well for Daisy. She overheard someone say that Marissa was going on a trip soon and would be gone for a few weeks. Daisy could hardly wait. But for the moment, just the sight of Marissa way up front, at least six rows away, filled her with relief.

Marissa, however, did not seem so pleased. She twisted around in her seat and swished her ponytail back and forth as she stared at Daisy.

Daisy was thinking about recess. She wished she could stay inside and read a book. She eyed the over-stuffed bookshelves, reading the titles, even the ones that were upside down. She could read upside down as easily as right side up. Since she'd finished her spelling assignment so quickly, Ms Kirby let her take a break. There were no copies of *Mary Popper and the*

Magician's Potion. A computer game would have to do.

Daisy walked down the hall to Mrs Brawnley's room. A computer game sounded fun. She slipped the disc into the computer and started the game. As she was trying to decide whether the prince should go up the tower steps or down the tunnel, she heard a whirring sound behind her.

"Hi, Daisy!" It was Cody's rusty metallic voice.

Daisy didn't answer. Great! The only one who is nice to me is a creepy robot-kid.

"Wow! You're at level five? I can't get beyond three," Cody said.

"Hmmm." Daisy shrugged. She heard the wheelchair back away.

Cody returned to the younger kids across the room.

Daisy felt relieved, but also a little disappointed. All that buzzing and clicking was weird, but Cody seemed nice. Unlike some other kids.

Five minutes later, her break was over. It was time for recess. Daisy stood at the window. Cody put a game away and then wheeled over to her. They gazed out at the other students.

"I hate recess," Daisy muttered.

"Me too," Cody said. "I used to like it. I used to play kickball and I was pretty good. Last year I kicked the ball right over that storage shed down there." He pointed at the far end of the field. "It landed in the middle of the Christmas tree farm."

"Really?" Cody was so skinny and frail-looking, Daisy could hardly believe it. "I thought you were a new student like me," she remarked.

"No. I've been here since kindergarten," Cody said. "Except for a while after my accident. I missed a year of school."

"What happened?"

"The accident? Oh, I was stupid. I took my brother's dirt bike for a ride." Cody fiddled with the controls of his wheelchair and it rolled back and forth. "It was getting dark and I was going fast, really fast, down this track through the woods. Wasn't even supposed to be there, you know? Definitely not on my brother's dirt bike!" He barked out a sharp laugh.

Daisy thought it sounded like a robotic dog. She squirmed.

"Anyway, there was a chain across the track. I never even saw it. So…" Cody slashed his finger across his throat. He stopped talking for a moment, gathering his breath. "The doctor said I was lucky. And I guess I am, in a way. At least my head's still attached."

Daisy felt dizzy at the thought of an unattached head. Ughh! She tightened her grip on the bookcase under the window.

Cody continued. "The hospital was so boring. But it was loads better than the next place I went – SODADD. That has got to be the worst place of all."

"SODADD?" Daisy echoed. "You went to the School of Disabled and Developmentally Delayed?"

"You know it?"

"I know it all right! I was there for a while." Daisy grimaced.

Cody shook his head. "Wasn't it awful? I called it the School of Doom and Despair. It was so bad one day I just couldn't take it any more. I told Mom I was going to pull out my tube if I had to go there one more day."

Daisy didn't know what to say. She plucked a tissue from the box on the shelf and began shredding it. Bits of white drifted to the floor.

"Cody!" Someone called from the hallway. "I'm going to get a cup of coffee. I'll be right back."

"Okay, Mom."

"That's your mom? I thought she was a classroom aide," Daisy said.

"She's both, sort of. She helps out in this classroom and she also makes sure my equipment keeps working."

"Oh."

"Well, I guess I better get ready to do my laps around the track. Mom always makes me go out and exercise." Cody snorted with disgust. "Wheeling around! Some exercise – it's so boring!" He headed over to the doorway.

"Yeah, I'm supposed to go out there too."

Cody shoved a knob forward and zoomed off. "See you later, Daisy!"

"See you later!" Daisy hung back in the doorway, checking over the playground. No Marissa in sight. But she could be lurking anywhere. Daisy decided to go back to Ms Kirby's room.

A minute later she walked over to Buster's cage. "Hey, Buster, how are you doing?" She poked a baby carrot through his cage. He made little shnuffling grunts as he nibbled the crisp treat. Daisy stroked his ears. "Today I'm going to get out to my special place, Buster. Mrs Brawnley told me I could go there. You'd like it there. It's quiet and the grass smells really sweet." Buster shnuffled some more. "And there's all these teensy little creatures out there – grasshoppers and gophers. Lizards. Once I even saw a little spotted snake. He was sunbathing on a rock and he blended in so well he was practically invisible." Daisy glanced around. "That's what I have to do – blend in."

Standing up, she grabbed her lunch bag. "Bye, Buster." She peered around the doorway. Where were those Bully-Pops? It took her a moment to spot them. Oh, good! They're way over at the swings! And there's a bunch of kids jogging around the track – probably training for the Jog-a-thon.

As the runners passed the classroom, Daisy darted over to join them. When they reached the far end of the track, she ducked behind a bushy shrub. Keeping her head down, she skittered up and over a dirt bank and down to a small grassy field. Her special place.

Daisy sighed as she sat down with her back against a stump. She propped her chin in her hand and leaned forward to see what she could see. A line of ants scurried by, carrying raisins. A brilliant tiger swallowtail butterfly fluttered around the willow trees. Daisy opened her snack container. Nibbling on strawberries, she eyed a gopher hole. Something moved in the shadow. A gopher poked his head out, spied Daisy, and yanked it back inside. "I wouldn't hurt you, little guy," she assured him with a smile. She leaned back and closed her eyes. So peaceful…

A pebble rolled down the bank behind her. Daisy looked up and squinted into the sun. Four dark figures stood above her. The Bully-Pops! She jumped to her feet, sending berries flying in all directions.

"Get back, you, you ghoulies!" Daisy stammered. "Get back or…or…or I'll throw a curse across your miserable hearts!"

For a moment the Bully-Pops just looked at each other. Then Marissa yelled "Get her!"

Daisy bolted across the field. But the Bully-Pops swooped down on her like a flock of squawking, pecking crows. As she tried to escape, she stepped in a gopher hole. She fell so hard she could hardly catch her breath.

"Oopsy, Daisy!" someone shouted. Laughing, they circled Daisy. She struggled to her feet.

"Ring around the Daisy!" Marissa sang. "We all know you're crazy! Clumsy and crazy! It's time to fall down!"

Marissa leaped close and *bam*! Daisy punched her in the nose. There was a loud squishy crunch. "Owwww!" Marissa collapsed on the ground, screeching.

Daisy screamed too. "Oh, Jeepers! Oh, Jeepers!"

Clutching her nose, Marissa stared at Daisy. Daisy stared back. "You punched me in the nose!" Marissa shrieked.

"I know! I punched you! I can't believe I punched you!" Daisy shrieked back.

"Aghhhhh!" She covered her face with her hands and scrunched her eyes closed. Everything seemed way too wild right now.

The Bully-Pops backed away. The screaming was fairly deafening at close range. They could hardly hear the bell ring. Then they raced off, their voices shrill even in the distance. "...fight! Daisy White... Marissa Thornton!"

In a few moments Daisy and Marissa were alone. Daisy sobbed quietly. Marissa still sat on the grass, rocking back and forth, holding her nose. "I think you broke it!" She groaned. "It's squashed flat as my mom's mushy pancakes." She glared at Daisy. "What are you whimpering about? I'm the one with the busted nose!"

"You're right, Marissa." Daisy agreed, her eyes still closed. She sniffled. "Why aren't you crying?"

"Huh!" Marissa said. "I'm not a baby."

Daisy gulped a few big breaths and stopped crying. "Well, I'm not either. Is your nose bleeding?" she asked, keeping her eyes squeezed shut.

There was some wet sniffling.

"Is it?" Daisy peeked, her nose wrinkling up. The mere thought of blood made her want to puke. But all she saw was Marissa's fingers spread across her wet flushed cheeks and her nose poking out. It was runny-looking, but not bloody. Cautiously, Daisy let her hands creep away from her face. "I don't see blood."

"Yeah, well, it still hurts! A lot!" Marissa muttered.

"I'm sorry, Marissa. So, so sorry." Daisy said. "I'm not a violent person. Really! You have to believe me! I know it was wrong to hit you. It was wicked and… and –"

"Okay, okay." Marissa interrupted her. "You're sorry."

"I'll never do it again. I am sorry with all my heart. Something evil must have possessed me. Ohhh, noooo!" Daisy wailed. "Something's taken over my brain!"

"Daisy, will you just hush!" Marissa stood up, still gingerly patting her nose. She trudged across the field and disappeared over the dirt bank.

Daisy sat hunched over, trembling. In a minute, Mrs Brawnley found her.

She knelt in the grass next to Daisy. Remembering how Daisy had once told her that sudden touches made her skin feel twitchy, she slowly put a hand on Daisy's shoulder. "What happened, Daisy? You look so upset."

Daisy told her what happened.

"Oh, Daisy, you are certainly not possessed," Mrs Brawnley assured her. "You are just a kid who's had enough of being bullied. You just lost your temper. I do wish we had known how difficult things have been between you and Marissa." She gently squeezed Daisy's shoulder. "I'll talk to Ms Kirby. We'll work it out."

"You mean I'm not going to jail?" Daisy asked.

"No, of course not." Mrs Brawnley smiled and hugged Daisy. "But I think Mr Sears will want to have a talk with you and Marissa."

"He will?" Meeting with the principal sounded pretty scary. Mr Sears always seemed so nice, but...he *was* the *principal*. Daisy shivered.

Chapter 4

The Principal's Office

Daisy sat in a chair in Mr Sears' office. He wasn't there yet. She plucked at the tissue Mrs Brawnley had given her, pulling it to bits and rolling the bits between her fingers until they made squishy little tissue pills. Frowning at the mess she'd made, she stuffed the bits into the crack of the chair's cushion. She leaned back and took a deep breath. The leathery material felt cool on the back of her legs. She glanced around. Everything looked tidy and well dusted. The yellow roses in the vase smelled nice, though they drooped a bit. A photo of a lady in a floppy hat sat on the desk.

Daisy huddled in the big chair, her feet dangling. What's he going to do to me, she wondered.

Mr Sears strode in and sat down at his desk. "Hi, Daisy."

"Hi, Mr Sears. How are you today?" Daisy straightened up and held her hands in her lap. Stay calm, she told herself. Be polite.

"I'm fine, Daisy. Thank you. How are you?"

"Very fine," Daisy blurted out. That's what her mom had taught her to say.

"Very fine?" Mr Sears raised his eyebrows. "But I understand you and Marissa are having problems." He leaned forward, frowning a little. "Tell me what's been happening."

Daisy told him about the Bully-Pops and the teasing and chasing.

"Oh, Daisy, I wish you'd told us sooner."

"But it's not good to tattle on your friends, Mr Sears," Daisy said, tears shining in her eyes. "Everybody hates tattle-tails. I just want to be a good friend."

"Daisy, they are not behaving like friends. Maybe they're not your friends."

"Yes, they are," Daisy insisted. "I think. Ohhhh, I'm so confused." She pushed her hair off her sweaty face. "Mr Sears." She took a deep breath and forced herself to look right into his eyes. "They are my only friends. No one else even talks to me – they just stare at me." Daisy sniffled. "Marissa used to be nicer. She's the good one. All the other kids like her." Daisy tried to get things straight. Her voice got louder. "I'm the bad one. I'm the violent one."

"Daisy, you are a wonderful person. You just made a mistake."

"How can I be a wonderful person? I punched Marissa in the nose!" Daisy shouted. "You're not making sense, Mr Sears."

He tried to comfort her, but Daisy was very upset. "You're confusing me," she cried. "I can't be good *and* bad. I hurt Marissa – I'm bad!"

"But Daisy, everyone gets angry sometimes." Mr Sears tried to explain. "People make mistakes all the time. Nobody is perfect."

"No. That's ridiculous. I don't understand." Daisy rocked back and forth, sobbing. "I wish I was a normal kid. I wish my brain wasn't weird." Her voice kept rising. "It's not fair! Why can't I be like everybody else?" Suddenly, she began pounding her head with her fists.

Mr Sears grabbed her hands. "Daisy, I can't let you hurt yourself. I'm going to hold your hands until you calm down. Okay?"

"Okaaaay!" Daisy yelled. She cried for a few minutes, then stopped and took a deep breath. She looked up at Mr Sears. "I'm okay now. I'm calm."

"That's good, Daisy. I knew you could get control again." He released her hands, giving them a gentle pat. "We'll work this out. The first thing I want you and Marissa to do is to write apologies to each other. Will you do that?"

"Sure, Mr Sears. Thank you for your kindness."

"You're welcome, Daisy." He nodded. "Are you ready to go back to Ms Kirby's class or do you think you need some time with Mrs Brawnley?"

"I'm okay – I'll go back to class." Daisy stood up and hugged Mr Sears.

He looked a little surprised, but then he smiled.

"Just one more thing, Mr Sears."

"Yes, Daisy, what is it?"

"Could you order me a new brain?"

Mr Sears' face changed. His gentle smile curved down into a worried-looking frown. He stared at Daisy. "Uhmm, Daisy, I...uhmm...you know I can't..."

Daisy stared back at him. "Mr Sears, I was just joking. I know you can't order a brain."

"Oh, of course." Mr Sears' face relaxed and he chuckled. "Very funny, Daisy."

Daisy laughed too, thinking it was funny that a grown-up like Mr Sears didn't even know when he was being teased.

The next morning, right before class, Marissa shuffled over to Daisy and dropped a piece of paper on her desk. "Here." She started back to her own desk, way at the front of the classroom.

"Wait." Daisy pulled a sheet of paper out of her backpack. "Here, Marissa." She held the page out, then snatched it back. "Oh, dear. Oh, no. It got wrinkled." She started smoothing it out, pressing and rubbing until the paper tore. "Oh, no. I'm sorry, so sorry, so—"

"Just give it to me, would you, Daisy?"

"No, I'll write it over. It's a mess."

"Like it really matters!" Marissa snatched it away from Daisy and marched back to her desk. A minute later she had her nose down staring at Daisy's letter. The letter was pretty short. It said:

Dear Marissa,

You shouldn't torture me. You make me scared and all nervous. I didn't mean to hit you. Really. You are my friend. I wish. Or maybe you are my archenemy. I'm confused. Is your nose okay?

Sincerely, Daisy White

P.S. Why do you always make up those rhymes?

Marissa's letter was even shorter. It said:

> Dear Daisy,
>
> I am wise, so I'll apologize.
>
> I won't bother you anymore — it was getting to be a bore.
>
> Yours truly,
>
> You Know Who

Daisy didn't know what to think. Did this mean that Marissa would stop bothering her? She didn't get to find out that day because Marissa's mother picked her up at recess and she was gone the rest of the day.

That night Daisy's mother and father stayed up late. Daisy couldn't sleep so she listened. She could hear her name come up often, but the few bits and pieces she heard didn't make much sense. Finally, she got bored with the jumble of words and fell asleep.

And the next day everything changed…

Chapter 5

Hampton Sweeney's Tongue

Right after the recess bell rang, Ms Kirby offered Daisy a special treat. "How would you like to take Buster out for a little fresh air and exercise?" she asked. "There's a perfect protected place right over there." She pointed to a nearby lawn enclosed by a small fence. "I'll be correcting some papers in the classroom so if you need anything…"

"Sure!" Daisy smiled and nodded. This sounded wonderful! Picking up Buster, she snuggled him close and rubbed her cheek on his fur. It was softer than anything. She hummed softly to him as she carried him out to the quiet grassy area. She set him down. He began nibbling the sweet grass. Daisy plucked a yellow dandelion bud and held it out to him. Buster reared up and took it, munching happily.

Daisy sat down on a big tree stump and held out another bud. "Come on, Buster… Hop up here," she coaxed. And he did. Soon a few kids noticed the rabbit. Daisy watched them approach. It's okay, she assured herself. It's okay. It's just Hampton Sweeney and his friends.

"Hi, Daisy," Hampton said.

"Hi, Hammy." Everyone called him Hammy. He didn't seem to mind. Daisy thought he was nice. She kept stroking Buster.

"What's Buster doing out here?"

"He's just out for a little fresh air and exercise. He gets bored in that cage, you know," Daisy explained.

"Yeah, I guess so." Hammy agreed, stooping down to pet him. "Hey, Buster! You having a good time out here?" He sat down, cross-legged and pulled a snack bag out of his sweatshirt pocket. He tore open the bag of chips and pulled out a few. His mouth opened wide, showing a huge, wet, pink tongue and lots of yellow teeth. *Crunch*!

Daisy ducked her head and edged away.

"Here, have a chip!" Hammy said, his mouth full of crumbly brown mash.

"No thanks!" Daisy said loudly. She yanked at the grass, concentrating on not looking at Hammy's messy mouth.

The other kids stepped back and began walking away. "See ya!" they called.

Hammy held out a chip to Buster. "Here you go, fella. Try this."

"No!" Daisy said. "Don't give him that. That's junk food."

"But this is healthy junk food," Hammy protested. "Look what it says right here." He held up the bag. "Thirty percent less fat than other chips! And it's made with whole grains and stuff."

Grabbing her backpack, Daisy whipped out her latest book, *Everything You Need to Know About Your Pet Rabbit*. "It says right here rabbits should not be allowed to snack on junk food."

"What? Where does it say that?" Hammy wiped his greasy fingers on his jeans and leaned closer to Daisy. A couple of crumbs stuck to his mouth. His hot, salty, stinky breath blasted Daisy in the face.

Daisy scrambled to her feet and turned her back to him. "Hammy! Would you go away now? Please!"

"Sure." He got up and traipsed away, muttering to himself.

Daisy turned to watch him, her shoulders slumping. Hammy was nice, but why did he have to talk with his mouth full?

"Hi! Can I pet your bunny?" someone asked.

It was a girl with bright orange hair. Really curly and wild.

"Sure." Daisy said. She had noticed this girl before. She liked the way the sun lit up her hair – neon orange. "Sure, you can pet him."

"What's his name?" the girl asked, kneeling next to Buster.

"His name is Buster. He's from Ms Kirby's class. She asked me to watch him."

"Oh. Hi, Buster." The girl rubbed him behind his ears. He stretched out his neck and closed his eyes. He looked blissful. "Feels goood, huh, Buster?" she crooned. "My name is Laurel. I'm a sixth grader in Mrs Macabee's class."

Daisy glanced over to see if the girl was talking to her or to Buster. Laurel smiled at her. Daisy looked away.

"What's your name?" Laurel asked.

Daisy remembered how her teachers told her she needed to look at people's faces in order to look friendly. She would like to be friendly to this girl. Daisy squeezed her eyes shut and took a deep breath. She forced herself to look at Laurel. "My name's Daisy. Daisy White. I'm in Ms Kirby's class."

"Oh, I had her last year. Isn't she nice?" Laurel commented as she settled into a more comfortable position.

Daisy checked to see if Laurel was going to be eating anything. It didn't look like it. Daisy sat down too.

"I used to have a wonderful white bunny," Laurel told her. "His name was Cotton. But one day my little brother left the gate open."

"Uh-oh," said Daisy. She wished she could think of something else to say.

"Do you have any pets?" Laurel asked.

"No. My dad has allergies. He gets these sneeze attacks," Daisy explained.

"Bummer," Laurel said. She tucked her hair behind her ears. "We have a zoo at our house – dogs, cats, parakeets, chickens. My brother has a gopher snake – he feeds it baby mice." She frowned. "Poor pink little hairless blobs."

"Yuck. That's awful," Daisy muttered. She twisted some blades of grass, keeping her eyes down. As Laurel began describing all of her pets, past, present and future, Daisy listened and smiled. She made herself glance up now and then, but mostly she kept her gaze away from Laurel's face. Faces could be so distracting and confusing.

As Laurel talked about all those pets, Daisy imagined a house with animals hanging out every window. Kitties, monkeys, a huge fluffy dog. And a yard overflowing with frolicking ponies, lambs, pygmy goats, pot-bellied pigs, and every kind of fun farm pet you could imagine. "That sounds fabulous," she told Laurel. "Tell me some more animal tales. Do you have any exciting ones?"

"Hmmm." Laurel tickled Buster's belly as she thought. "Oh, here's one. Jimmy, my little brother, he caught this big old king snake last spring." Laurel stretched out her arms as wide as they'd reach.

"Longer than this. And so big and strong that it could rear up and push the top off its cage."

"Wow!" Daisy quit pulling on the grass and sat up straight.

"So, Mom told Jimmy he had to let it go – and he was going to, but he kept saying 'one more day'. Anyway, right then my Auntie Bea arrived for her spring visit. Now, Auntie Bea is really nice, but kind of proper, you know. Older people get like that – and she's at least forty or fifty."

"What do you mean – proper?" Daisy asked.

"Like…all prissy and polite. Clothes freshly ironed – no wrinkles. Hair just so."

Puzzled, Daisy eyed Laurel's hair.

Laurel patted her unruly red curls and batted her eyes. "You know – just like mine." She snickered.

"Anyway, Auntie Bea has poor circulation and she gets chilled real easy. So we always turn up the heater in her room to make sure she's nice and cozy." Laurel paused. Her eyes narrowed into a sly look. "She likes animals and all, but she's kind of squeamish around a certain species."

"Snakes?" Daisy said. Her toes wiggled. This was getting exciting.

"Yesssss!" Laurel started making these snorty laughing noises. "Anyway, she wanted to change out of her traveling clothes and take a nap before dinner. And…" Laurel paused to take a breath.

"And what? What happened?" Daisy giggled nervously. The story was giving her the jitters. Thrills ran through her fingers making them flutter.

"She pulled back the bed covers and – guess who else likes it all warm and cozy?"

"Oh, no!"

"Yep! There he was all curled up in her bed – this enormous snake!"

Daisy's eyes opened wide. "What'd she do?"

"She screeched like a parrot being plucked – loud enough to make our dogs all start barking and then…" Laurel pounded the grass, choking with laughter. "Then she came flying down the stairs, still squawking – with nothing on but her underwear! Everything was all flopping and jiggling. And her underwear – it was bright red!"

"No!" Daisy whooped, kicking her feet so they drummed on the lawn.

Daisy and Laurel laughed so hard that Buster stopped nibbling and turned to stare at them. As they chatted, they found out they liked a lot of the same things. They both were crazy about dogs, especially small cuddly ones. Neither of them cared much for fish, but they both liked snakes. Except for the feeding part. They both loved *The Incredible Journey* and they both hated the ending in *Old Yeller*. "Sad endings are unforgivable," Daisy declared. Laurel agreed.

Daisy had been having such a pleasant time talking with Laurel, she'd almost forgotten all about the Bully-Pops. But now, as they sauntered over, whispering and cackling, she felt her stomach begin to squeeze. Laurel ignored them. The Bully-Pops stood around for a while, but finally Marissa flipped her fat ponytail over her shoulder and turned away. "C'mon, there's nothing but a couple dumb bunnies around here," she huffed. And they left.

When the bell rang, Daisy was sorry to say goodbye to Laurel. This was the best recess she'd ever had.

After school that afternoon, Daisy's mother commented "You look happy – did you have a good day, Honey?"

"Very fine, Mom." Daisy paused. Then she smiled with her whole face. "Actually, it was wonderful!"

"Really?" Her mom stopped rooting around in the refrigerator and looked over at her.

"Yes! Two things happened. One, I found out Marissa's going to be gone for a few weeks. And, two, guess what else! I have a friend – a great new friend." Daisy dumped her backpack on a kitchen chair. "Her name is Laurel and she's really nice. Very funny, too."

"That's great!" Her mom poured some chocolate milk in a cup. She set the cup down on the table next to some oatmeal cookies. Daisy always had milk and cookies after school. "Tell me all about this new friend."

So Daisy did. When she finished describing Laurel and all her pets and funny stories, she stood up, carefully patting the crumbs off her mouth with a paper napkin.

"I can't believe it, Mom! My first real friend."

"You had friends at your old school," Daisy's mother remarked.

"Yeah, right!" Daisy said. She started pacing around the room. "All Micky ever talked about was doorknobs. What kind of conversation topic was that? And Bryan – he never talked at all."

"What about Robin?" her mother asked as she wiped the table.

"Mom!" Daisy stopped pacing and planted her hands on her hips. "She moved to Illinois!"

"Oh. Well, then… I guess you're right, Daisy."

"I am absolutely right, Mom," Daisy insisted.

"Yes, you are – absolutely one hundred percent correct." Her mom smiled at her.

"Why'd you have to remind me of my old school, anyway? You know I hated it!" The bad memories all of a sudden seemed like they had just happened.

"Daisy, I'm sorry." Her mother wasn't smiling now.

Daisy slammed out of the house and up the path to the playground where she threw herself belly-down on the inner tube swing. She pushed herself around, winding the chain up and then letting go so the swing twirled her like a spinning top. Why'd her mother have to remind her of SODADD? But SODDAD reminded her of Cody. All of a sudden she wanted to tell her mother about Cody.

She ran back into the house. "Mom, I almost forgot – I have two new friends."

Her mother stopped chopping carrots. She looked up. "Really? That's great!"

Daisy told her all about Cody, then added "Actually, I almost have three friends. Hammy's nice but I can't stand the way he chews. And he knows nothing about proper nutrition for rabbits."

"Hmmm." Her mother smiled as she pulled apart some lettuce leaves.

"I love you, Mom."

Her mom wiped her hands on a dish towel and placed her hands on her hips. She put on her silly-serious look and corrected Daisy. "No, I love YOU."

"No, I love YOU." Daisy argued back, giggling.

"I love YOU!" "I love YOU!" "Love-you-love-you-love-you! YOU-YOU-YOU!" They rocked and hugged and laughed at their own silliness. Most of the time my mom is really all right, Daisy thought. A little goofy, but all right. This was turning into a very good day.

And tomorrow would be even better.

Chapter 6

Scritchy-Scratchy Noises

The next morning Daisy brought Buster out again. I bet Marissa's plotting some more tricks, she thought. She kept looking over her shoulder. The Bully-Pops were nowhere in sight. But Daisy quickly spotted that whirl of bright orange hair. Laurel was talking with a group of other kids. She waved at Daisy.

Daisy waved back, beaming.

The other kids turned to look in Daisy's direction. Then they huddled around Laurel, their heads bent close, whispering. Suddenly, Laurel walked away from them, saying something in a loud and kind of annoyed way. Daisy thought it sounded like "…I don't care!"

In a minute Laurel stretched out on the grass next to Daisy. They chatted about animals again as they fed Buster his treat of the day – baby carrots. "Buster is such a cool classroom pet – our class just has this lizard. All it does is lie there. It practically looks dead," Laurel complained.

"You think *that's* bad?" Daisy said. "At my last school, my class just had this dopey goldfish. All he did was float around dangling this long green string of poop. And, after Bryan threw the fishbowl on the floor, we didn't even have *him*!"

Laurel laughed and asked "What school did you go to?"

Daisy didn't answer at first. Laurel waited.

"Mitchum Avenue Elementary," Daisy finally said. She fiddled with her bracelet.

"Oh. Where's that?"

When Daisy explained it was down the hill and across town, Laurel wanted to know why she had to go to such a far-away school.

"I was in a special class, the autistic class there. But don't tell anybody, okay?" Daisy said.

"Why don't you want people to know you're artistic? I think that's great!" Laurel said in a bubbly voice. She rumpled up Buster's fur, then smoothed it down again. "A special class for artistic kids! Cool! So, what's your favorite medium? Paints? I love watercolors!"

"Paints?" Daisy looked puzzled. "What are you talking about art for? I'm no good at art!"

"But you just said you were in this artistic–"

"No – I was in a class for AW-tistic kids," Daisy explained. "You know, for kids who have autism."

"Autism? What's autism?" Laurel asked.

"Well, it's hard to explain. It's like, umm…there's a variety of things…" Daisy looked up at the sky as though the right words hung there in the clouds. "It's like something that you're born having and it may run in your family – like your aunt or uncle might have it. Your way of seeing the world and other people is a little different than most people's."

"I still don't understand," Laurel said, shaking her head. "You seem pretty much just like any other kid to me. You don't look any different. How are you different?"

"Well, for one thing," Daisy said – she held up her pointer finger –"I get mixed up with what I'm doing and where I'm going sometimes." She paused and held up another finger. "Two, sometimes I don't understand slang. You know, slang words? Like… well, this morning my dad was in a hurry, right? And I couldn't find the sweater that goes with my pants, and I was standing there thinking about what to do because that's really important, you know, to have things match, right? – oh!" Daisy interrupted herself. She took a deep breath and held up another finger. "That's another thing. Everything has to balance out and match right. It has to. Anyway, my dad said 'Daisy, come on! Look alive, Kiddo!'" Daisy paused to glance at Laurel.

Laurel looked back and shrugged. "So?"

"So? Look alive? I mean, I was standing there with my eyes wide open. I was breathing. Of course, I looked alive." Daisy shook her head in disgust. "What a stupid thing to say. Why didn't he just say it the right way? Like if he meant hurry up, just say, hurry up."

"Okay, I think I understand."

Daisy barely heard her. She was getting excited now. "Oh yeah, here's a big one – I have to have things a certain way, the right way. I hate changes and surprises. I hate almost any food that I haven't tried before, which is almost everything. Smells drive me crazy."

"What smells?" Laurel asked as she rubbed her arm, making a raspy noise on her windbreaker.

Daisy winced. "And scritchy-scratchy sounds! They hurt my teeth!"

"Oh! Sorry!" Laurel stopped scratching.

"Smells? You know, smells like Chinese food or gasoline or things like that. Any strong smells. And loud noises – those really freak me out! Like in crowds when people start clapping. Oooh..." Daisy shuddered and took a deep breath. "Sometimes I get so wired I have to run around and flap my hands – I'm trying to learn to control that because some of my teachers told me other people think it's really weird." Daisy twiddled with the figures hanging on her bracelet. "People don't notice finger flicking as much."

Laurel rolled over and gently tugged Buster onto her stomach. "But lots of people get lost or like matching clothes. That's not so different. And I don't like loud noises myself, so I still don't see what's so different about people with autism."

Daisy was quiet for a moment. "Well, probably the main thing about autism is that it makes it hard to be with other people. You really want to have friends, but it's too hard."

"What's too hard?"

"Being a friend is too hard."

"Hmmm."

"You don't get it, do you?" Daisy asked impatiently.

Laurel shrugged, tickling Buster's neck.

Daisy leaned forward. "You see, there are different degrees of autism. Some autistic people have like this thick brick wall that separates them from everyone else. They can't even talk." She reached over and pulled a bit of note paper away from Buster. "I guess I'm sort of lucky because I just have Asperger's."

Laurel looked shocked. "What? Tell me you didn't just say you have ass boogers!"

"I didn't say ass boogers," Daisy said, sounding irritated. "I said Asperger's."

Laurel's nose wrinkled. "Ass burgers? Daisy, that sounds even worse. What are you talking about?"

"A-S-P-E-R-G-E-R-S. That's the name of the guy who sort of discovered us."

"Oh, I get it," Laurel said. "So this, Asperger's thing. What exactly is it?"

"It's autism that's not as bad as the brick-wall kind. It's more like a flimsy paper screen between me and everyone else. Sometimes, I can almost reach right through it." Daisy sighed wisfully. "Sometimes."

"Oh."

All of a sudden Daisy scrubbed at her eyes. The skin around them turned purplish pink.

"I'm sorry, Daisy. I didn't mean to upset you." Laurel bit her lip as she watched tears gather in Daisy's eyes.

"It's not your fault." Daisy sniffled. "It's just another thing about autism – I get upset really easily."

They were quiet for a moment, then Daisy asked Laurel "Do you think I'm weird?"

"Not any weirder than a lot of other kids."

Just then Michael Duffy walked by making incredibly loud sticky-armpit farts. *Bffffft! Bffffffft!* "See what I mean?" Laurel said.

They both giggled. Daisy wiped the tears off her cheeks and started talking again.

"Anyway, about schools? Before I went to SODAD, I was at a class for kids who can't talk right, but I can talk. Obviously! And then there was the class with these really hyper kids. They were so wild." Daisy wrapped her arms around her knees and began to rock back and forth. "This one kid kept screaming all the time. He wouldn't stop until I threw my chair at him."

Laurel's eyes got wide. "You threw your chair at him?"

"I know...it wasn't the best way to handle it. That's when I got transferred to SODADD, the School of Doom and Despair. That place is too awful to even describe. That wasn't where I belonged. No way! I belong here – with the normal kids." Daisy stopped rocking for a moment. "I think."

Laurel was quiet. After a minute she said "I think you belong here, Daisy."

"Really? Do you think so? Are you sure?" Daisy looked right into Laurel's eyes.

"Yeah, I know you do." Laurel smiled at her.

Chapter 7

The School of Doom and Despair

The next day Daisy was on her way out to the lawn with Buster when she heard an argument.

"But Mom! I belong *here*! They can't send me back to SODADD!" The voice was squeaky and the speaker kept coughing so badly it sounded like he was choking.

It was Cody, Daisy realized, as she paused outside Mrs Brawnley's room.

"It'll be better this time, Cody. They've opened up a new class for high-functioning students."

"No! I won't go and that's it!"

Something rammed the other side of the door with a horrible bang. Daisy opened the door and Cody burst out full-speed. His wheelchair ran over Daisy's foot.

"Ouch!" She almost dropped Buster. For a few moments she hopped around, moaning. "Jeepers, Cody!"

Cody zoomed down the hall.

"Hey!" Daisy yelled. "That's a hit and run! That's against the law!"

Cody disappeared around a corner.

"Some friend he is!" Daisy muttered as she limped away. "People are so strange, Buster. Even Laurel. I haven't seen her lately." She stopped and frowned. "I wonder if she's avoiding me."

Daisy carried Buster out to the lawn and put him down. She stroked him, but he was in a rowdy mood and didn't hold still for long. He scampered around the lawn and leaped over a low-growing hedge. In a minute he was next to Daisy again. "Buster, you are such an athletic bunny," Daisy told him as he stretched out in the shade. "And you're smart. I bet I could teach you some tricks."

Buster flicked his ears and lay quietly. His pink tongue poked out a little. He was hot. Daisy poured some fresh water into a small plastic bowl. She had decorated it with bunny stickers so it wouldn't get mixed up with any other bowls. Buster lapped at the cool water delicately, like a cat. He made the tiniest splashes and got some sparkling droplets on his whiskers. In a few minutes, he was romping around again.

Daisy got out his favorite berry treats. She encouraged him to jump up on this low beam that edged the lawn. As soon as he did, she praised him in a high chirpy voice and gave him a treat. Buster got the idea quickly. In a few minutes, he'd learned to leap up on one end of the beam, hop along the length of it, and leap down off the other end.

Daisy was so busy with Buster that she didn't notice a few kids had wandered over to watch. "Hey, that's pretty cool how you're training him," one of them remarked. Daisy turned around. It was a group of sixth graders – Laurel's friends.

"Yeah. Thanks," Daisy replied, ducking her head. "Has anyone seen Laurel?"

"She's been sick with the flu the last few days," one of the girls said. "I talked on the phone with her last night. She says she'll be back tomorrow."

"Oh. I hope so," Daisy said, glancing up at the girl.

"My name is Annie," the girl said. "Where'd you learn about animal training?"

Daisy was telling Annie about her Aunt Rosie, a professional animal trainer, when the bell interrupted her.

"See you tomorrow!" Annie called as she hurried off to class.

Daisy scooped up Buster and trotted off to her own classroom. She felt bouncy and light. "Laurel wasn't avoiding me, Buster," Daisy whispered. "She was sick!"

The next day Laurel was back at school. "Hi, Daisy!" she called, strolling over with Annie and some other kids. "I hear Buster's learned a cute trick. Can I see it?"

"Sure!" Daisy grinned. "Up, Buster! Up!" she commanded in her best bunny-trainer voice. She made a sharp motion with her hand as she stood next to the wooden beam. Buster leaped up, bounded along the beam, and jumped down at the end. "Good boy!" Daisy praised him. She cuddled him and gave him a blackberry. "Good boy!"

"Wow! That is awesome! I never knew rabbits could learn tricks like that." Laurel was impressed.

"Buster's brilliant," Daisy said, stroking his velvety fur. "He's easy to train."

"Annie told me your aunt is an animal trainer."

"Yeah. My Aunt Rosie trains dogs and horses," Daisy explained. "She taught me a few things when I went to visit last summer."

"Are you going to teach Buster any more tricks?"

"Sure! I think."

Later that afternoon, Daisy crouched next to a bench in front of the school, waiting for her mother to pick her up. She was looking at a blue-belly lizard basking next to the grapevines when she heard a whirring sound.

"How's your foot?" a familiar raspy voice asked.

"Oh, hi, Cody. It's fine."

"Good." He rolled back and forth restlessly. "I'm waiting for my mom to come out. She's in a meeting."

"I'm waiting for my mom too." Daisy paused, strumming at her backpack straps. "Why are you going back to SODADD?"

"I'm *not*." Cody shook his head. "No way! Never!"

"Well, you don't have to get mad at me."

"Daisy, I'm *not* mad at you. Honest." He coughed. "I'm just so…so…"

"Upset?"

"Yeah. I'm really upset. But there's nothing that can make me go back there," he said fiercely.

"Alright already. You already said that – don't repeat yourself."

"Well, excuse me!"

"Well, it's okay. Do you want a cookie?" Daisy pulled a few slightly crumbly cookies out of her back-pack.

"No, thanks."

"Come on," Daisy insisted. "It'll make you feel better."

"Oh, all right." He took one and nibbled at it.

"You look glum," Daisy told him.

"Glum? *Glum*? Where do you get these words?" Cody snorted and made a little harsh barking cough.

"Mostly, they're in the dictionary. Some, like snorf, I get out of my brain."

"What's snorf?"

"It's when you snort and cough at the same time."

"Of course," Codie smiled. "I knew that."

They munched on the cookies. Daisy gave Cody a paper napkin and told him to wipe some melted chocolate off his chin. "So, if you're not going back to SODADD, why are you upset?" she asked.

Silent, Cody gazed out at the mountains to the west of the school. The hills rolled away to reveal a long forested valley which opened out to the ocean. It was a clear day and you could almost see the whitecaps on the bright, blue water. Finally, he said "I don't know what I'm going to do. See, my mom needs to go back to work. She can't be my aide at school any more."

"Why not?"

"She needs to find a regular job."

Daisy sprinkled some cookie crumbs around and watched as a few ants began to carry them away. "Why do you need an aide, anyway?" she asked.

"Well, just in case I have a problem. Sometimes my breathing machine gets fouled up."

"But why can't the school just get another aide?"

"That's what Mom's meeting Mr Sears about. The problem is that the aide needs special training and it costs a lot," Cody explained. "Some people say I should just go back to SODADD."

"*What?*" Daisy jumped to her feet and stood in front of Cody with her hands on her hips. "But that's not right. *This* is your school!"

Cody shrugged.

Daisy grabbed his shoulders. "Jeepers, Cody! You belong here! Don't allow the powers of darkness to discourage you!"

"Take it easy, Daisy!" Cody pushed her hands away.

"But Cody, you're practically my best friend. You're almost my only friend! It would be totally dismal around here without you." Daisy started pacing back and forth, her fists clenched. "We must gather the forces of goodness. We shall overcome this evil!"

"Daisy, I think you've been reading too many of those fantasy sci-fi books. You're beginning to sound just like Mary Popper."

Daisy narrowed her eyes at him. "Cody, we are discussing your future fate. And all you're worried about is criticizing my linguistic patterns?"

"I wasn't being critical about your, your...whatever you said," Cody apologized. "I'm glad you care. Really. But how are we going to do that thing...you know, that overcoming the evil thing?"

"How? Who knows how?" Daisy said. "But we'll think of something." She plopped back down on the bench and stared out at the distant sea. "We have to."

"Well, we better think of something fast. My last day here at Ocean Vista is the day before Thanksgiving," Cody said.

"Don't worry," Daisy assured him. Then she frowned. "How long is it until Thanksgiving anyway?"

"About four weeks."

"Oh, that's plenty of time. We'll figure out something." Daisy stood up, snatching her backpack. "There's my mom. Have a good weekend, Cody."

Cody blew out a puff of air, whistling slightly. "Yeah, right."

Chapter 8

The Sad Stranger

For the next few weeks, Daisy worried about Cody. As she worked in class or munched her lunch or sat in the car on the way to Aunt Rosie's, Cody was always in the back of her mind. How can I save him from SODADD? How, how, how, she asked herself. But the answer wouldn't come.

The only time she wasn't wrestling with Cody's problem was when she was playing with Buster. She taught him to stand on his hind legs and beg for a blueberry. Then she borrowed a hula hoop from Mrs Sullivan, the gym teacher. Soon Buster learned to jump through the hoop. She taught him to weave through a line-up of posts – soon he could zig-zag around them like lightening.

Buster enjoyed all the play and attention. One day he did his very own wildly happy performance. Daisy had just put him down on the lawn when he began leaping about, twisting and bucking his hind legs in the air like a floppy-eared, puffy-tailed little bronco. He danced around, jumping high and corkscrewing through the sunshine while Laurel and Daisy watched, astonished.

"What is he doing?" Laurel asked. "My rabbit never did anything like this!"

"I read about it in my rabbit book. It's what rabbits do sometimes when they're really happy and excited," Daisy answered, her fingers fluttering. She was really happy and excited too.

"He looks so funny!" Laurel chuckled. "Yeah, Buster! Go, boy! Go!"

After a few minutes, Buster hopped over to a patch of shade and stretched out to rest. Daisy crouched next to him. "Buster! You silly guy! I didn't know you could jump like that!" She and Laurel grinned at each other.

"What are you going to teach him next?" Laurel asked.

"You'll see." Daisy trotted into Mrs Sullivan's office and returned with a huge rubber ball. She had an idea. Could Buster do it? She held him over the ball and lowered him until his paws just touched it. Carefully, she nudged the ball with her toe. It rolled slowly and Buster moved his paws, taking tiny hops. The ball kept rolling and Buster stayed on top for a foot or so before jumping off. After some practice, he rode that rolling ball all by himself.

"Wow! He's like a circus bunny or something!" Laurel said. "This is fabulous!"

By this time, Buster's stunts attracted a crowd of kids at every recess. Daisy was beginning to relax and enjoy recess. No one had teased her in a long time. She would have been perfectly happy, except Cody's predicament kept pinching at her mind. Think, she told herself. You've got to think of something.

One day, as she was thinking about Cody, she heard some laughter, that ugly, nasty kind of laughter that she used to dread. It was the Bully-Pops. They were surrounding a girl that Daisy didn't recognize. The new girl wore glasses and had a huge bandage over one eye. She stood with her head down and shoulders drooping. Then Daisy overheard someone say "Oh, don't be so touchy, Marissa."

"Marissa?" Daisy stared. Oh, no! Marissa was back! Just when everything was going so well! But this girl didn't look like Marissa. She didn't act like Marissa either. But, as the other kids ran off, tittering, Daisy could see that it *was* Marissa. She certainly didn't look very scary today. Unless mummies made you nervous. That bandage was big.

"Wow! Look at Marissa!" Daisy said to Laurel. "I wonder what happened to her."

"She had to go to San Francisco and have eye surgery. There's something wrong with her eyes," Laurel said.

"What? How do you know that?"

"Her big sister is friends with my big sister. They were talking about it."

"Oh." Daisy cocked her head and continued to study Marissa. "Her body language indicates possible depression." She pursed her lips. "That's not good. I know about these things, Laurel."

Laurel shook her head and laughed. "Yeah, Dr Daisy, you might say it kind of funny, but you're right. She does seem pretty bummed out. Wouldn't you be? I mean, she has to wear those dorky glasses for…well, forever. Probably."

"Really? What about the bandage? She won't have to wear that forever, will she?" Daisy looked worried. "I wonder if there's blood underneath there."

"Probably."

"Yuck." Daisy shuddered. "Poor Marissa."

"Poor Marissa? Wasn't she being awfully mean to you?" Laurel reminded her.

Daisy thought about this for a moment. "Yeah. But now some kids are being mean to her. I heard them. Look. She's sitting over there all by herself."

Laurel shrugged and tried to change the subject. "I heard you're teaching Buster a new trick."

"Yep! We're working on a see-saw ramp now and...and..." Daisy's voice trailed off as she continued to gaze at Marissa. "Will you watch him for a minute? I'll be right back." She hurried off without waiting for an answer.

"Okey-dokey," Laurel murmured.

"Hi, Marissa!" Daisy called to the girl slumped on the bench. "How are you doing?"

Marissa didn't look up "How do you think I'm doing?"

"Oh. Not so great, huh? Does it hurt under the bandage?"

"No, not if I stay quiet. If I move around too much, it starts to throb. But mostly, it's just a big bore." She heaved a huge sigh and swung her feet back and forth, scuffing up little puffs of dust.

"Your new glasses look nice."

"Ha!" Marissa snorted. "If you think that, you ought to be wearing glasses yourself! The lenses on these are as thick as the cruddy old bottles my granny collects. They're awful! One of my so-called friends just told me I look like a bug-eyed cyclops."

"Really? Let me see." Daisy bent over, trying to peer into Marissa's face.

"No!" Marissa buried her face in her hands. Her shoulders started to shake.

Daisy stepped back, shocked. "You're crying."

"Yeah. And I'm not supposed to cry. It's bad for my eye," Marissa mumbled, sniffling.

"Well, at least you can still rhyme," Daisy said, as she patted Marissa on the shoulder.

Marissa sat up, shrugging off Daisy's hand. "I'm trying to stop. It's a habit. I got it from my mom. She's in therapy because she has lots of habits she needs to stop."

Daisy was silent for a moment, then she grabbed Marissa by the hand and tugged her to her feet. "I know what will cheer you up. C'mon!" She led Marissa over to the little yard where Buster and Laurel waited.

"Hey, where're you taking me? What're you doing?" Marissa grumbled. But she didn't pull her hand away from Daisy's. After watching Buster perform a few stunts, she said "He's cool. That rabbit is definitely cool." She almost smiled.

Chapter 9

Daisy and the Really Great and Truly Wonderful Idea

One day, while Buster and Daisy were entertaining some friends, Ms Kirby walked over to them. "Daisy," she said, "How would you and Buster like to represent the school in a special pet show? It's a big school fundraiser. All the schools around this area are entering their classroom pets – there'll be rats and turtles and who knows what else. There'll be lots of prizes." She paused. "Even a grand prize for the most amazing pet."

Ms Kirby smiled at the children. "And the class who wins the grand prize gets a large cash award for their school. Why don't you think about it, Daisy?" She strolled away.

Daisy was scared about the idea. A show meant lots of people…lots of noise…lots of confusion and commotion. Nope. She didn't want to do it.

"Come on, Daisy! You have to do it!" some of the kids said. They were excited. "You and Buster could win the grand prize – you're definitely amazing!"

"No, thank you. Really. I don't want to." Daisy was getting all hot and jittery just thinking about it.

"C'mon, Daisy! Say you'll be in the contest!" the kids urged her.

"No!" Daisy yelled so loud Buster dashed off and hid in some bushes. Most of the kids backed away. Hammy trudged over to coax Buster out of his hiding place, while Laurel talked to Daisy.

"Daisy, it's okay if you don't want to be in the contest," Laurel said.

"No, it's not! Everybody's going to hate me now."

"No, they won't. They're just disappointed, but they'll still like you."

Daisy didn't believe her. How could something so wonderful turn into something so dreadful! She was going to lose all her friends! What should she do? "I have an idea!" She stood up and grabbed Laurel by the arm. "You can be Buster's trainer!"

"It's an idea, Daisy, but not really a good one," Laurel said. "You know Buster listens to you way better than anyone else."

Daisy didn't say anything. She knew Laurel was right.

The next day Daisy didn't even feel like bringing Buster out.

"Where's Buster?" Laurel asked.

"He's taking a break today." Daisy slouched over to a bench and sat down.

Laurel followed her. "Hey, Daisy. I checked with my mom. She said you could come over this Saturday. Do you want to?"

Daisy looked up. "Sure. I guess so. Do you mean it?" She didn't get invited to a friend's house very often.

"Well, of course. You can see all my pets. It'll be fun."

Daisy felt like smiling again. "That sounds super. Totally super."

Just then Marissa joined them. "Hey, Daisy! Guess what! I get my eye patch off tomorrow."

"That's great, Marissa!" Daisy hugged her.

Marissa laughed and pushed her away. "Hey, where's Buster? Doesn't he need his fresh air and exercise?"

"Yeah, I guess he does." Daisy brought him out and everything seemed back to normal. Kids came over to chat and play with Buster. No one said a word about the pet show. Yet Daisy felt something twisting inside of her. Something wasn't right. Cody. She hadn't seen him in a few days.

After her homework that night, she asked her mother where the Ocean Vista phone directory was. "I need to call Cody," she explained.

She dialed the number. "Cody?"

"Who is this?" the voice said.

"Daisy White."

"Oh, hi, Daisy. This is Cody's mom." She hesitated. "Well, Cody's not feeling… Oh, well. Maybe he'll talk to you. Just a minute."

"Hi, Daisy." Cody's voice sounded even more raspy and deep than usual. Totally Darth Vader.

"Hi! Why aren't you in school?"

"Why bother? I'll be leaving soon anyway."

"No, you can't leave. You–" Daisy started to say.

The phone clicked. I guess he doesn't want to talk about it, she muttered. Suddenly, she didn't want to think about it. A scary thought kept squirming around in the back of her mind. She slammed the phone down.

How to save Cody from doom and despair? There's a way you can do it. You know what you have to do. Nope! It won't work anyway. I don't have to! I can't! She ran outside, trying to push the idea out of her mind. She scurried up and down the garden pathway, yanking the leaves and flowers off of every plant she passed. Until the rose bush.

"Ouch!" She sat down and cried, sucking on her finger. It stopped bleeding, but she continued to sob. What should I do, she wondered. The thought of performing in a show sent her heart into a galloping panic.

Later that night Daisy talked with her mom and dad at dinner. She explained about the pet show and how Buster could win the prize money to pay for a new aide for Cody.

"I know I can't be in the pet show, but I really don't want to let my friends down either, especially Cody," she said, as she pushed her peas around her plate. She was so nervous just thinking about performing that she couldn't eat a bite of dinner. She slumped in her chair. "I know I'd just freak out and make a total fool of myself."

"I can understand how you feel, Daisy," her mom said. "To be up there with everyone watching – it's…it's a really challenging kind of experience."

Her dad nodded. He was kind of a shy person himself.

Daisy's mother continued talking as she cut a piece of pot roast. "Of course, you were in your class musical performance – you enjoyed that quite a lot."

Daisy poked at her potato. "That was way different, Mom! I wasn't the only one up there. And I knew just what to expect and what to do. There's no rehearsal for the pet show, you know."

"That's true, Honey."

For a few minutes, there was just the clink of silverware and other quiet mealtime sounds.

Daisy put down her fork and gazed at her mother and father. "Do you think I can do it?"

"Of course, you can," her dad said quickly. Too quickly.

"Dad, don't talk with your mouth full!"

He rolled his eyes. "It wasn't full."

"You had food—" Daisy started to say, but her mom interrupted.

"If it really means a lot to you, Daisy – and I know it does – you can do it. We can just prepare for it like we prepare for other challenging situations." She started buttering a slice of bread.

"Really?"

"Absolutely!" Slathering on some more butter, her mom continued. "We could visit the school where the show is going to be and figure out how things are going to look and sound and what you'll be doing. And we could set up Buster's performance so you wouldn't be up there alone. Your friends could help with some of it – you know, bringing out the props and things. We could have our own private rehearsal." The layer of butter was getting very thick.

"With a little preparation, you'll do fine!" her dad said, winking at her.

Daisy started smiling. Her fingers did their happy dance. "Can I be excused? I want to call Cody! And Laurel! Marissa, too!" Daisy dashed down the hallway. "But first, Mr Sears!"

A moment later she dialed and got Mr Sears' answering machine. "Mr Sears? Are you there? This is a matter of urgency! A student's fate is in your hands! Call me immediately or sooner if you can." She waited, then hung up. After a second she called back. "Yours truly, Daisy White."

She called Laurel next, then Marissa. "Awesome idea, Daisy! We'll help you," they assured her.

"Cody's going to be so excited," she murmured as she dialed his number. "Cody, listen to this! I thought of something!"

"Listen, Daisy…" Cody didn't sound excited the way he should. "Thanks for trying to help me, but –"

"You haven't even heard my idea yet!" Daisy said. She explained what she had in mind.

At first, Cody said nothing. Only the breathy hum of his machine filled the silence. Then he spoke and, for the first time in a while, Daisy heard a flicker of hope in his voice. "Buster does have some awesome tricks, Daisy…but, even if you win, it doesn't mean the prize money will go for training an aide. The school needs money for all kinds of stuff. Why would they spend the money on me?"

"Don't worry, Cody. Saving you from doom and despair is the most important thing. Everyone knows that."

"Daisy, you're a great friend. No matter what happens, I'll always remember how you tried." Cody hung up.

The next morning Daisy raced into Mr Sears' office. "Did you get my message? Why didn't you call me back?" She paused, out of breath. "Mr Sears?"

The principal turned and put his hand up. He was on the phone. "Just a minute, Daisy."

In a few moments he hung up. "I just got your message a little while ago. Why don't you sit down and tell me what this is all about."

Daisy described her plan.

Mr Sears listened with his hands leaning together like a church steeple. "Hmmm, I think your idea is wonderful, Daisy, but I need to talk to some other people about it. I don't make the money decisions by myself."

"Promise you'll try your best?" Daisy reached out and grabbed his hand.

"I promise."

Daisy hurried out of the office to find her friends. They needed to practice for this pet show. Laurel set up the low beam, Marissa rolled out the big red ball and Hammy was in charge of hauling out the see-saw. Cody held the hoop and Daisy gave Buster his voice commands and hand cues. They were a great team.

A week before the show, when Daisy's mom drove her over to the site of the pet show, Laurel came along. They walked around the community center with the pet show coordinator. She showed them where they would wait and when their turn would come They talked about what to expect – laughter and clapping and lots of kids and pets milling around. And they found a secluded place for Buster and Daisy to go if the commotion got too intense.

Daisy still felt nervous, but she kept telling herself "I can do it. I know I can do it. I have to do it for Cody."

As the day of the pet show drew closer, Daisy and Buster practiced until the clever rabbit could do his tricks easily. Cody, Laurel, Marissa, and Hammy rehearsed too. They moved out to an area where lots of people could watch so Buster could get used to the sights and sounds of the crowd. The whole school buzzed with anticipation. Buster and Daisy were sensational!

Then, two days before the pet show, something terrible happened.

Chapter 10

Time of Trouble

It was right before recess ended. An old dirty pick-up truck drove over and stopped in the parking lot near the grassy area where Buster was performing. Two teenagers sat in the truck. One jumped out. He held a bag in one hand and, with the other, hung onto a black and white dog. All of a sudden, he released the dog. He yelled something to it and pointed to Buster.

As the dog rushed over, Daisy tried to snatch up her bunny. But Buster was already dashing away with the dog right behind him.

"No! No!" Racing after them, Daisy yelled so loud her throat hurt. "Stop it!" Visions of Buster torn to bloody pieces flashed through her mind. She had to get to him before the dog did!

The other kids stampeded around the lawn, trying to save Buster. The rabbit and the dog darted back and forth. This way – that way – this way – that way! The children chasing after them leaped in so many directions so fast that they slammed into each other and tripped over one another. Marissa and Daisy collided head-on. *Bam*! Daisy sat stunned. She rubbed her forehead. "Jeepers."

Marissa jumped to her feet and charged back into the chase. Her new glasses were trampled into the grass.

The dog herded Buster right over to the boy with the truck, but Marissa sprinted after them, her ponytail flying out behind her. The boy pounced on Buster and tried to shove him in the bag. Marissa yanked at the boy's arm and shrieked loud enough to blast his eardrums. She slowed him down a bit with her determined tussling, but as Daisy reached the scene, the boy and the dog bounded into the truck. With a loud squealing noise, it sped away.

Daisy, Marissa, and some other kids chased after it, but it spun around the corner in a cloud of dust and was gone. And so was Buster.

Some of the kids were yelling. Some cried. Betsy Yamato was so upset she got the hiccups. Daisy stood staring after the truck.

Laurel ran over to her and hugged her. "Why?" She sobbed. "Why would anybody want to kidnap a rabbit?"

A few teachers rushed over. "What happened? What's going on?" they asked. Then Mr Sears hurried out to the crowd of kids.

"Who's been kidnapped?" he yelled, yanking out his cell phone. "Buster who?"

"Daisy's Buster! You know, the rabbit!"

"Oh, Buster the rabbit." He put the phone down, looking relieved. "But you guys are all okay?"

"No! We're – hic! – not okay!" Betsy gasped. "They took – hic – Buster!"

"I know you're all upset," Mr Sears said. "Let's try to calm down and we'll see what we can do." He listened to their story and then asked "Can any of you describe the vehicle?"

Several children shouted at the same time.

"It was a pick-up truck!"

"A green truck!"

"A blue truck!"

"Okay. Good. It was a truck." Mr Sears said. "Did anybody see the license plate?"

"I saw it!" Hammy said, all excited.

"Well, what were the numbers on it?"

"Oh, ummm, something like…ummm…" Hammy mumbled. "Oh, I don't know – it was hanging loose – swinging practically upside down – I couldn't read it."

Everyone groaned with disappointment.

"Can anybody remember anything else?" Mr Sears asked. "Anything at all?"

Daisy wiped the tears out of her eyes and spoke up. "I remember some things," she said. "The boy with the dog wore a red and black checkered shirt. He had shaggy blonde hair. I think his dog was a border collie. The truck had a big dent on the back fender."

She paused to gulp for breath. She still felt all shaky.

"That's very good," Mr Sears said, looking slightly surprised.

Daisy continued. "There was a bumper sticker that was half torn off – it said something 'is cool.' And the license plate was hanging loose, just like Hammy said." She added, "The number on it was BJ8 113."

Astonished, Mr Sears asked "Are you sure? How did you manage to see all that?"

"Marissa slowed him down enough," Daisy explained. "She got there first and kept him busy so while I was running across the lawn I could see everything."

"It's true, Mr Sears," Hammy said. "Daisy practically has laser vision and once she sees something, she doesn't forget it."

"Yeah, I've seen her read an encyclopedia – upside down," Marissa said.

Daisy repeated the license plate number. "I'm sure that's it."

"Way to go, Daisy!" a few kids cheered. "Way to go, Marissa!"

"With all that information, the police just may be able to track them down." Mr Sears tapped in a number on his phone. "I'm calling them right now. You guys head back to class now, okay? I'll let you know what's happening."

Back in the classroom Daisy sat down at her desk and laid her head down. The lump on her forehead throbbed. The desktop felt good against her hot cheek. Poor Buster, she thought. What are they going to do with him? She was so worried she couldn't think of anything else.

Then someone tapped her shoulder.

"Daisy, I'm really sorry about Buster," Marissa whispered. "I tried to get him back."

"I know. Thanks for trying." Daisy looked straight at Marissa's face and squinted. "You've got a bump the size of a goose egg on your forehead."

"Yeah, and you've got one as big as…as big as…well…it's really big. I think you better wear a wig."

Ms Kirby interrupted them. "Daisy? Marissa? I can see you've got some nasty-looking lumps. Please go to the nurse's office immediately."

A few minutes later, they sat on a bed holding ice packs to their foreheads. Sniffling, Daisy peeked out at her friend. "Marissa, you look funny."

"Daisy, your nose is runny." Marissa giggled.

Daisy gave her a crooked smile. Marissa and her silly rhymes.

After school, Daisy went home feeling so sad that she could hardly lift her feet. She told her mom what had happened. "Buster's gone and Cody's doomed!" she wailed.

Her mom hugged her and tried to cheer her up, saying "They'll find Buster, Honey. He'll be okay. And so will Cody." That night she made Daisy's favorite dinner – bunny-shaped pasta with cheese sauce. Daisy's throat felt choked so tight she could hardly swallow.

Later, her father tucked her into bed like he used to when she was very little – with the blankets nice and snug around her. It felt good to be wrapped tightly. Somehow that feeling of heaviness pressing around her made her feel secure, like a bunny tucked safely in his burrow. Soon Daisy's breathing slowed and she slept.

Daisy felt peaceful. She and Buster were out in a sunny meadow. She was weaving a crown of dandelions for him. As she called him over to put it on his head, she heard a horrifying howling in the distance. It got louder and louder. Something was coming. The ground began to shake. The sky darkened. Then a pack of huge wolves raced towards Daisy and Buster, their dripping fangs snapping and yellow eyes glowing! Daisy grabbed Buster and tried to run, but she kept falling. She couldn't breathe! Something was tangling her legs. She kicked and thrashed desperately. The wolves hurtled towards them. Closer and closer.

Just as they were about to tear her and Buster to bits, Daisy sat up, gasping for breath.

Her dad was shaking her shoulder. "Daisy, wake up, Honey."

What a dreadful dream!

Suddenly she remembered what had happened yesterday – the real nightmare. Poor Buster! Where was he? Was he okay, she wondered miserably. Daisy untwisted the blankets and stumbled out of bed. Her throat was dry. She got a drink of water and splashed her face. What could she do to find Buster?

Chapter 11

Bunny in the Brambles

Daisy dressed and joined her parents for breakfast, although she didn't feel much like eating. Her dad was reading the newspaper, as usual. Then, he suddenly set down his coffee cup and sat up straight, reading intently.

"Daisy, look here! There's an article in the local news about Buster. They found the guys who kidnapped him."

Daisy dropped her toast. She listened as her dad quickly read the rest of the article. The boys had heard about Buster and didn't want him in the pet show. One of them owned a large boa constrictor that was part of a music and dance performance. He wanted his younger brother to enter it in the show and he was worried people might like Buster's act better than his snake's.

"Oooh!" Daisy's mother shuddered. "He was probably right about that."

Daisy's father continued. "The police officer in charge of the case said the only reason they were able to find the kidnappers so quickly was because of the truly amazing power of observation shown by the missing bunny's trainer, a student at Ocean Vista Elementary School." Smiling proudly, he paused to look at Daisy. "That's you, my dear – the Amazing Daisy."

Daisy had been holding her breath. Finally, she couldn't wait any longer. "What about Buster?" The words burst out of her.

"Let's see… Oh, it says the boys claim that they did not harm the rabbit. They let it loose in Pine Meadow Park. That's over on the far end of Hilltop Road."

"Oh, Dad, take me there. Take me there right now," Daisy begged. "Please?"

Her father looked like he was going to refuse, but then, he and her mother looked at each other. "Well, I guess you wouldn't be able to concentrate at school today anyway." He put down the newspaper. "Let's go."

Ten minutes later Daisy and her dad walked across the wet grass at the park. "Buster! Buster!" they called.

The park looked deserted. Nothing moved. They poked around some bushes. A little brown bird flew out, twittering nervously. Then a gardener arrived and unloaded a lawn mower. In a few minutes it was roaring.

Daisy clapped her hands over her ears. She felt like telling the man he was scaring off Buster. I just have to keep looking, she told herself as she searched the picnic area. No Buster; just a few ants eating crumbs. Daisy and her father walked around the playground. They checked under the slide and around the swings. Nothing. Daisy called until she was hoarse, but the loud drone of the lawn mower drowned out her voice.

Finally, her father looked at his watch. "Well, Honey–" he began.

"Dad, please? Can't we look a little more?"

"Daisy, we've been looking for almost an hour. Buster could be anywhere by now." Her dad tried to reason with her.

At that moment the grass mower stopped. It was quiet enough to hear a squirrel chatter in an oak tree next to them. Now's my chance, thought Daisy. "Buster!" she shouted, feeling desperate. She had just started calling him when several cars pulled into the parking lot. Mothers and toddlers and babies spilled out all over, laughing and scolding and squalling. Daisy felt like screaming for them to be quiet.

"C'mon, Daisy. We'll come back with the posters," her father suggested.

"But that'll be too late, Dad! Anything could happen to Buster out here – a coyote could eat him! A car could hit him! All kinds of things!" Daisy argued. "Just one more minute, please?"

Without waiting for his answer, she ran over to a tower and began to climb. The metal was so cold it made her hands ache. The steel steps under her feet were slippery. Her shoes made a loud pinging noise as she climbed up to the top. She held on to the railing and studied the park below. At first, she saw nothing. Then, she spotted a faint trail through the grass. Some little animal had run – or hopped – and disturbed the pattern of dewdrops sparkling on the grass blades. The tracks led up a steep bank and into some blackberry brambles.

"I see something!" Daisy clattered down the steps, calling to her father. "Dad! I see something!" She scrambled up the slick bank and over to the brambles. As she knelt down, she heard a rustling.

"Buster?" she whispered.

All of a sudden, a little furry animal hustled out of the shrubbery.

A ground squirrel.

"Ohhh, why couldn't you be Buster?" she asked it as it dove into a hole. Her disappointment made her whole body droop.

Her dad jogged over. "Just a squirrel, huh?"

"Yeah." She eyed the thorny bushes. It did seem to be the kind of place a bunny would like to go. "Buster!" she called softly, leaning into the shadowy tangle of brambles. Something moved deep inside the blackberry patch. "Wait. I hear something."

She strained forward, peering into the darkness. It was silent. Her hands pressing down on some sharp pebbles began to hurt. She pulled back, then realized the thorns had snagged her hair. As she tried to pull loose, they pricked her fingers and face. "Ouch!" She felt ready to cry.

Her dad crawled in next to her and untangled her hair. They both backed out. He blotted the scratches on her face with a tissue. "It's probably another squirrel, Honey. C'mon, we've done our best here."

Daisy was not convinced. "We can't just give up. We've got to do something."

"We can go home and make some 'Lost Rabbit' posters," her dad suggested. "Then we'll come back and put them all around this neighborhood, okay?"

Daisy sighed. "Okay…" Dragging her feet through the wet grass, she walked with her dad across the lawn and back to their car. She turned to take one last look. Squinting against the glare of the early morning sun, she stared at the brambles. The moist leaves and thorns shone so brightly her eyes watered.

All of a sudden, something leaped out of the shadows — a dark silhouette with long ears. Daisy's heart began to pound like crazy. She blinked. "Buster?" She grabbed her dad's arm. "Dad! Look!"

"Buster!" she shouted joyfully, running to the rabbit. But as Daisy got near him, he dashed back into the bushes. Staring after him, Daisy could see he was smaller than Buster and brown — not black. He was just a little wild brush bunny.

"You're not Buster! You stupid rabbit, why'd you fool me like that?" Daisy cried. "I want my Buster!" She grabbed a twig and threw it into the thicket.

"Daisy, it's okay." Her dad hurried over and hugged her. "We'll find Buster."

Daisy collapsed against him, sobbing. "What if it's already too late?"

"Listen, Honey, we need a plan, right?"

"Right. I guess."

"Let's go home and work on the posters, okay?" Her dad slid his arm around her shoulders and they walked back to the car.

That afternoon Daisy and her dad and Laurel pinned posters around Pine Meadow Park and up and down Hilltop Road. Marissa and Hammy stuck some up on the side streets in their neighbourhoods. And Cody and his mother put up some on the bulletin boards at the market and the veterinarian's office.

The posters looked like this:

MISSING BUNNY

BLACK AND BEAUTIFUL AND VERY SMART

BIG REWARD FOR FINDING BUSTER,
THE WORLD'S BEST BUNNY

CALL DAISY AT 343-3589

P.S. YOU MUST FIND BUSTER NOW!

After traipsing around putting up posters for hours, Daisy was very tired. She almost dozed off at the dinner table and was too worn out to even take a bath. She dragged herself upstairs, kicked off her shoes, and dropped into bed with her clothes still on.

The sun had not even slipped behind the ridge yet. Although she fell asleep quickly, she didn't stay asleep.

Something woke her.

Chapter 12

By the Light of the Moon

When Daisy opened her eyes it was dark, except for the faint glow of her nightlight. She had heard something. What was it? There it was again – the sound that pulled her out of her exhausted sleep. It was an owl hooting, a Great Horned Owl.

"Oh, Buster," she whispered. "I hope you're hiding deep, deep, deep in the brambles where nothing can get you." She snuggled under the blankets and tried to go back to sleep.

"Whoo-Whoooo!"

Daisy pulled the pillow over her head. Her breathing sounded loud inside her ears. She was too hot. The same blankets that seemed to snuggle her earlier now seemed to strangle her. The zipper on her sweatshirt kept snagging on the sheets. They made an awful scritchy-scratchy sound. Daisy thrashed around, twisting and trying to get comfortable. She finally got her sheets straightened out, but she was thirsty. She groped around on the nightstand for her glass of water.

The glass was empty. Slipping out of bed, Daisy padded across the room and downstairs to the water cooler. As she stood at the window sipping the icy water, she stared into the darkness and thought of Buster and Cody. Both of them are doomed unless I do something. But what?

The clouds drifted away from the full moon and a brightness filled the yard. Moonlight made the chrome metal on Daisy's bicycle sparkle like polished silver.

As Daisy eyed her bike, an idea formed in her mind. Buster is at the park, waiting for me. I know he is! He just couldn't hear me calling this morning. But it's quiet now. I could just hop on my bike and ride down the road to the park. Buster will hear me and come. I know he will. Thrilled with her brilliant plan, Daisy paced back and forth across the kitchen, thinking and flapping her hands with excitement.

Daisy glanced up the stairs. Not a sound from her parent's room. Mom and Dad wouldn't like this idea. The owl hooted again, making her flinch. I'm not even sure I like this idea. I'm not the world's greatest bike rider, but I guess I could walk my bike down that steep part of the road. Daisy rubbed her arms, shivering. It'll be all right. This idea will work – it has to!

Daisy slipped her feet into her shoes at the door. Quietly she hurried out and hopped on her bike. She grabbed the helmet that hung on the handlebars and put it on. Mom would be mad if I didn't wear this

clunker. She shoved off and pedaled down the driveway as fast as she could. Puffing hard, she rode down the narrow winding road.

The forest closed in on both sides like a tunnel of trees. Everything looked so different at night. What was peaceful and beautiful in daylight now seemed strange and threatening. Long strands of Spanish moss hung like ghostly hair from the huge branches of ancient oak trees. Their twisting branches seemed to reach out to grab her. Tree monsters, Daisy thought. "I'm brave, I'm fearless, I'm going to find my bunny!" she chanted, as she barreled through the gloom.

Here and there moonbeams shone through the branches, but mostly it was dark. When she hit a pothole, her bike jittered so hard she almost lost her grip on the handles. "Yikes!" she yelled. Shouldn't the park be right here? She slowed down.

Careful, she warned herself as she swerved around another pothole. Passing a meadow, she relaxed a little. It wasn't so dark along here. She coasted down a slope, her long hair waving in the breeze.

The fresh scent of grass and pine forest filled the air. Daisy took a deep breath. I can do this, she told herself.

Suddenly, something snorted loudly and a large dark shape bounded across the road in front of her. Gasping, Daisy slammed on the brakes. She heard the sharp smack of hooves on pavement and saw a flash of antlers. A deer. She'd almost run into a big buck.

She pedaled onward and spotted the old wooden water tower looming ahead. I'm almost there, she thought. I know I'm going to find him now.

"Buster!" she called. Her voice sounded loud in the hush of the mountain night. It made an eerie echo. "Buster!" "Usterrrrr!" the sound bounced back.

Daisy glided through the shadows and leaned into a curve in the road. Before she knew it, she was zooming down a hill. Fast, way too fast. She stamped on the brakes so hard her bike skid in the gravel.

"I'm brave, I'm fearless!" she shrieked. "I'm going to hit that treeeeeee!" Her bike flew over the edge of a steep bank.

Everything seemed to happen in a terrible slow motion. The wind whistled in her ears as she soared through the air. Daisy and the bike slammed into the ground, bounced, and tore through some bushes. Then, with a horrendous crash, the bike flipped upside down. After that it was quiet except for the sound of wheels spinning. In a minute, that noise stopped and it was very still.

Daisy lay on a pile of dead leaves. Her bike was on top of her. "Oh, Jeepers! Oh, Jeepers," she moaned, too shocked to move.

After a moment, she noticed a rattling. Heart pounding in terror, Daisy listened as the leaves around her rustled. The frightening noise surrounded her. What's that? she wondered. She took a deep breath, listening with all her attention.

As she lay holding her breath, totally motionless, the noise stopped. Daisy released her breath, still feeling very shaky. "That was just your own shivering, you silly goose," she told herself. She let out a little sobbing giggle.

Finally, her heart quit thumping so hard. She stared up at the sky through the handlebars. She could see the stars. They were whirling. She closed her eyes and tried not to throw up. Oh, Jeepers.

After a while, Daisy opened her eyes. It seemed like every part of her body was throbbing. She felt crushed under the bike. She pushed at it. Owww! Her wrists hurt. Especially the right one. Cradling her arms against her chest, she rolled over.

The bike tumbled off of her.

"I'm okay, I'm okay," she assured herself. Her teeth chattered and she shivered harder. She tried to stand up, but dizziness made her sink back down. The jerky motion of the shivers stabbed her wrists with pain. I've got to quit shaking, she told herself, got to get warm.

Groaning, Daisy squirmed around, trying to find a comfortable spot in the twigs and dry leaves. Dry leaves? That's it, Daisy. Scootch into the leaves until you're covered. She felt a little better just thinking of such a good idea. She wiggled around, careful not to jar her wrists. Soon she had a blanket of leaves over her. Better, she told herself. The leaves of the bay tree smelled spicy-sweet, but dusty and moldy too. She sneezed, making her wrists jerk. "Ouch! It hurts!" she whimpered. Then the pain forced her eyes and mind to close and she slept.

Minutes and minutes crept by. Daisy teetered back and forth between sleep and wakefulness. Once, as her eyes fluttered open, she felt something crawling on her arm. She froze. Just a bug, she whispered to herself. Don't look. It's just a little bug of some sort. But she did look. A large centipede scurried across her hand. She held her breath and silently begged it not to sting her. It didn't.

Daisy heaved a sigh of relief as it disappeared into the leaves.

I wonder when Mom and Dad will notice that I'm gone. Oh, Jeepers, maybe this wasn't such a great idea. At least I almost made it to the park. Raising her head, Daisy peered through the forest and saw a clearing just ahead. Yeah, there it is.

Then she heard a small noise in the underbrush nearby. Too big a noise for a centipede. Too little for a deer. Daisy hoped it was not a snake. Whatever it was, it was coming closer. The noise stopped.

Daisy lay listening, waiting. She was wide awake now. What was that noise?

Chapter 13

Lizards, Tarantulas, and Goats! Oh, My!

There it was. The rustle. Even closer now. Coming faster. As she listened, heart pounding, Daisy realized that there was a familiar rhythm to the sounds.

Hop-hop-stop.

Her eyes opened wide. "Buster?" she whispered.

A few moments later her bunny's whiskers tickled her face.

"Buster! You found me!" Daisy tried to hug him, but her wrists hurt too much. Tears leaked from her eyes, blurring her vision and dribbling down into puddles inside her ears. "Buster, I'm so glad you're here." She cuddled him close to her and waited for the sun to rise.

"Daisy!" The voices woke her up. "Where are you, Daisy?"

Buster skittered under a nearby log. "It's okay, Buster," Daisy called to him.

"Daisy?" It was her mother.

Daisy tried to shout loudly but her voice was weak. "Mommy!" she croaked. "Mom! I'm down here!"

A few moments later her mother's face appeared on the dirt bank above her. "Daisy!" Her mother slid down the slope, calling over her shoulder. "She's here! Right over here!"

"Mom, don't scare off Buster," Daisy mumbled. Then it seemed the sun set suddenly – a darkness swooped over her. She felt her dad's strong arms tenderly gathering her up and carrying her to safety.

When Daisy awoke, she was in a white room – a hospital. Her wrists were bandaged so she couldn't bend them. She ached all over. "Where's Buster?" she said.

"How do you feel, Honey?" her parents were asking, both at once.

"Very fine," she answered. "Where's Buster?"

"He's safe in his cage at school." Smiling, her mother stroked Daisy's face.

Her mother's hand felt so cool, so soft, like a bird's wing fluttering against her cheek. Daisy fell asleep again.

A few days later, Daisy returned to school.

When she walked into her classroom, everyone jumped up and ran over to greet her. "Way to go, Daisy! You found Buster! Are you okay?"

"I'm fine, totally fine!" Daisy said impatiently. She hurried over to check on Buster. He was fine too.

"I'm so glad to hear you're doing all right, Daisy."
Ms Kirby smiled. "Are you all set for tomorrow?"

"Tomorrow?" Daisy looked blank.

"The pet show," someone whispered.

"Oh, yeah! Silly me!" Daisy said. "How could I forget – the pet show is tomorrow." She felt a flutter in her stomach.

"You *are* still going to do it, aren't you?" Hammy asked.

Daisy glanced around the room – her friends were all waiting for her answer. Would she be in the pet show tomorrow? "Well…" she said.

The room got very quiet.

"Well, of course! Why wouldn't I?" she asked.

Everyone cheered. Daisy put her hands over her ears.

"Okay, boys and girls!" Ms Kirby called. "I know we're all excited, but we have work to do. Please get out this week's spelling list."

At recess Marissa brought Buster out. Daisy walked along with her friend. Her wrists were still sore. "I think we should just let him relax today," she said to Marissa. "He knows his routine – he doesn't need any more practice."

"He does look kind of tired," Marissa agreed.

So am I, thought Daisy. She went to bed early that night.

When she awoke, the sunshine was streaming through her window. "Today is the day," she said aloud as she climbed out of bed. She stepped into a pair of blue jeans and pulled on her favorite T-shirt. It was bright pink with bunnies dancing all over it.

She pattered downstairs and sat at the table.

"Daisy, are you sure –" her mother began.

"I'm fine, Mom. Absolutely fine. Laurel's going to do all Buster's handling while I do the voice commands. Marissa, Hammy, and Cody will do the props. It'll be fine. Really."

Nervously, Daisy sipped at her orange juice. "I don't want anything to eat right now, Mom."

"Okay, Honey."

Soon they were on their way to the pet show. When they arrived, it looked different, but Daisy knew it would. Kids, parents, and teachers milled around. And, of course, classroom pets of every kind, all extremely talented, Daisy suspected. Bunches of bright balloons bobbed at the ends of ribbons. Streamers blew in the breeze. And banners from the different schools made everything look festive.

Daisy spotted the banner with Buster painted on it – and right there under it were Ms Kirby and her class. And there was Buster, sitting in his cage, nibbling on a slice of apple. He seemed unfazed by all the commotion.

Daisy knelt next to Buster and stroked him. She said "If you can do this, so can I."

The show began. The first contestant was a white rat with brown spots. It raced through a fancy hand-made maze. The maze looked like a castle with dozens of hallways all leading to dead ends except for one. The rat found his way through and climbed up on a tiny throne to get his reward. There were loud cheers as his trainer carried him off-stage. Next to perform was a cockatoo named Einstein. He used his beak to flip through a book, then flew over and landed on one of the judge's shoulders. He leaned over and said "I can talk – can you fly?" As he cackled, he bobbed his head up and down waving his crown feathers. "Ha-ha-ha!" he croaked before flapping back to his trainer. Everyone roared with laughter.

After the cockatoo, a boy came out wearing a magician's outfit. He didn't have a pet, but he put on an act like he was looking for one. He peeked under a bench, behind a banner, and finally, he sat down at the table and pulled off his hat. He acted shocked when a huge tarantula crawled out of it.

Daisy thought Ms Kirby was going to faint.

The next contestant was a girl who led a little goat onto the stage. It was supposed to do some fancy stunt, but it got spooked and started bucking and jumping around. It ended up tying its trainer up so that she tripped.

Some people laughed. Daisy felt sorry for the girl. She leaned over to Laurel and whispered, "I hope we do better than that."

"We will," Laurel answered.

Everyone watched as the next contestant carried in a turtle. The turtle took a look around then pulled its head and feet into its shell. The trainer marched around it, waving a baton in time to some dramatic band music. The turtle refused to come out. After a few minutes the trainer scooped it up and, still marching and waving, carried it away. He got some disappointed clapping from his classmates.

"Well, at least he didn't lose his cool," Cody remarked. "I wonder what that turtle was supposed to do."

"There's just a few more before us," Marissa reminded them. They watched a couple of guinea pigs chase each other around and a large lizard who sat on its trainer's shoulder and occasionally flickered its tongue and blinked.

"Big deal," Hammy muttered. He tapped his foot impatiently. "I wonder if that boa constrictor is going to show up."

"Those guys wouldn't dare come!" Marissa said. "Oh, look who's up next!" She pointed to a slim, elegant Siamese cat that sauntered onto the stage. A pretty girl in a fancy frilly dress followed the cat. *Swish*,

swish, swish went her dress. With graceful flair, she flung out her arm and prompted the cat to begin his act. He climbed up a tall post and then trotted daintily across a very narrow flimsy board. The board flexed and bounced slightly.

"Wow! It's like a tightrope act!" Daisy exclaimed.

The cat's trainer dangled a wire with a realistic-looking bird on it. Leaping high, the agile cat twisted and spun, batting at the bird. As a finale, the girl had the cat jump up on a purple velvet chair and sing. "*Mwowllll!*" the cat wailed. "*Mwowlowlll!*" When he was done, he sat there with a smug look on his pointy little masked face.

The girl bowed and the audience clapped. The girl bowed again. The applause began to dwindle. Looking bored, the cat began to wash its stomach. As the girl started to bow again, someone called "Thank you, Susie! That's enough." Susie and the cat sashayed off the stage. *Swish, swish, swish.*

"It's our turn, Daisy," Laurel said.

Daisy felt like there were worms squirming in her stomach. Could she do this? What if she tripped over one of the props? What if she couldn't remember what to do next? What if Buster got spooked and ran off? What if? What if? What if?

Her thoughts ran wild like chickens chased by a fox.

Chapter 14

That's What Friends Are For

As Daisy waited for her friends to set up Buster's props, she took deep breaths. "We can do this, Buster," she told him.

Laurel picked up Buster and together Daisy and her friends climbed up on the stage. Cody gave her a big smile, Hammy gave her a thumbs-up, and Marissa whispered "Daisy White, you're all right!"

"Okey-dokey, Buster. Let's do it!" Daisy backed up a little, giving Buster a chance to check out where everything was.

They started their performance. "Beg for a berry, Buster!" Buster begged. "Jump the hedge, Buster!" Daisy pointed to a line-up of big boxes painted with leaves. Buster jumped over to the far side of the boxes, then jumped back again. Back and forth the eager rabbit bounded over the "hedge." "Let's do the hula, Buster!" Cody grabbed a hula hoop and held it out. Buster sailed through it.

There were some cheers and whistles.

Daisy directed Buster to a series of posts, set close together. "Zig-zag, Buster!" she said. He darted back and forth through the row of posts, his body twisting and turning.

More people applauded.

Daisy grinned at Buster. She was beginning to enjoy this.

Marissa rolled out the big red ball. "Have a ball, Buster!" Daisy said. Buster eyed it, his ears twitching. Then from a standstill, he leaped aboard the ball. Marissa released it and Buster hopped along as the ball rolled beneath him.

The audience cheered and clapped.

"Way to go, Buster!" Daisy rubbed his head and offered him a berry. "Just one more, fella!" Putting up her hand, she waited for silence. She motioned for Hammy to drag out the see-saw.

Buster didn't wait for Daisy's command. He raced over and hopped on to the lowered end of the see-saw. Then he scampered along the board until it tipped down on the other side. There he stopped and turned around. He crouched, waiting.

"Are you ready to fly, Buster?" Daisy asked. She nodded to Hammy who banged the end of the see-saw down with a resounding thump. Buster flew through the air directly into Cody's arms.

The kids in the audience jumped to their feet as they clapped wildly.

"Daisy White! You're all right!" Marissa started it, but soon everyone was chanting "Daisy White! You're all right!"

Daisy waved and hurried off to her quiet place with Laurel and Buster. She was very happy, but, suddenly,

it was all a bit much. She didn't watch the rest of the show. She even missed the awards, but after a while Cody, Marissa, and Hammy came to tell her all about them. The rat got the award for the smartest pet and the cockatoo got the award for the funniest. A mouse that kept popping out of its trainer's pockets and sleeves got the award for the cutest pet.

"Aren't you curious about who won the grand prize?" Marissa asked impatiently.

"Nope," said Daisy. "I already know Buster is the best."

"You're right!" Marissa hugged Daisy. "You and Buster did win! You were amazing!"

"Look at this, Daisy!" Hammy pulled a huge golden trophy from behind his back and held it out. "It's going to be engraved with our school name and everything."

"Very nice," Daisy remarked as she looked inside the trophy. "Where's the money?"

Her friends laughed.

The next morning Daisy was called to the principal's office.

Oh, no! What did I do, she wondered as she walked in. Cody was there too. And the golden trophy sat gleaming on the desk.

Mr Sears looked very pleased. "Daisy, your suggestion was considered and, I'm happy to tell you, it was approved. Cody's going to be staying here with us. You won the money to pay for his aide's training."

"Wow! That's great!" Daisy said. She was so happy her fingers tingled. "That's fantastic! Wonderful! Stupendous! Awesome!" She paused for breath. "Can I go now?" She turned to leave.

"Hey, Daisy." It was Cody. "You're the best friend anyone could ever have."

Daisy stopped at the door and glanced back over her shoulder. She smiled with her whole face and her whole heart as she looked right into Cody's eyes. "Hey, what are friends for?"

Author's Note

I wrote *Buster and the Amazing Daisy* for my son, Devon. Dev has Asperger's Syndrome, a condition on the autistic spectrum. He faced some big social challenges in his first year, mainstreaming in the regular classroom. I wanted to encourage him. As I read this story to him, I realized it would be so great to share the story with his schoolmates. In fact, it occurred to me that it would be really fantastic if other children, teachers, and families could hear this story too. So, here we are!

There are several factors that contributed to the happy conclusion in this tale:

- Daisy's teacher was patient and understanding. She taught the children to appreciate the uniqueness of each of us.

- Daisy was not punished for her outbursts, but given support to recover and learn a different way of responding to stress. She was allowed time and space to calm down.

- Daisy received support at recess – a quiet, "safe" environment and a special way of "connecting" with other kids through a popular common interest – a friendly animal.

- The school principal, teacher, special education staff, and parents worked as a team.

- An older student, matched to Daisy's interests, was enlisted as a "buddy."

- Daisy's parents understood how to prepare her for new situations.

I have found the following books, publishers, and organizations to be helpful in understanding and supporting my son:

- *Asperger's Syndrome* by Tony Attwood (London: Jessica Kingsley Publishers)

- *My Social Stories Book* by Carol Gray and Abbie Leigh White (London: Jessica Kingsley Publishers)

- Future Horizons – an organization that offers great books and conferences on autism

- Free Spirit Publishing – a publisher of many wonderful books for kids on every important topic you can imagine

- Parents Helping Parents – a non-profit organization that offers educational resources and support for parents of kids with special challenges.

Acknowledgements

A special thanks must go to Paula Jacobsen for her keen insights, helpful advice, and unflagging support. This project would have foundered without her.

Thanks, too, to Dr Linda Lottspiech for taking time to review my manuscript.

I'll be forever grateful to Oliver Niemann, a kind first friend to Dev, and Oliver's mother, Jean, an incredibly skilled and committed aide. Also many thanks to Dev's other wonderful aides, as well as to the students, teachers, staff, and principal at Loma Prieta Elementary School.

Thanks, too, to Nicky Tenney and Jack and Lynn Mullen for their careful reading of my manuscript and thoughtful suggestions. Also I greatly appreciate the time and energy put into reviewing this work by the parents of some "special" kids.

I thank my many marvelous friends who believed in me. Miriam, Pam, and Cindy, I most especially appreciated your encouragement.

Many thanks to my sister and brother, who cheered me down the final stretch of this project.

Finally, a big thanks to my family. Devon and Cory, your excitement about this book kept me writing. Last, but definitely not least, I thank my husband, Ron, for his patient technical support and for never complaining about the messy house and uncooked dinners. You put up with a lot, Honey!

Blue Bottle Mystery

An Asperger Adventure

Kathy Hoopman

Nothing is quite the same after Ben and his friend Andy find an old bottle in the school yard. What is the strange wisp of smoke that keeps following them around? What mysterious forces have been unleashed? Things become even more complicated when Ben is diagnosed with Asperger Syndrome.

Blue Bottle Mystery is great fun to read and will keep you guessing until the end.

'I read this book in under an hour and then immediately picked it up and read it again, much to my brother's disappointment ("It's my book!")… It was a wonderful to listen to his cries of "Oh now I under-stand," "I do that," "Aspergers – that's what I have." We shall have to buy another copy because both my brother and I love it too much to let the other have a read… Congratulations on a truly wonderful book.'

– Clare Truman (age 14)

Kathy Hoopmann is a primary school teacher and children's author who lives near Brisbane in Queensland, Australia. She enjoys camping, walking on the beach, and writing on the computer for hours on end. She is married with three children, two zebra finches, a cat and dozens of wild birds that feed on her back deck. Kathy has been involved with children with Asperger syndrome for many years.

ISBN 1 85302 978 5

Of Mice and Aliens

An Asperger Adventure

Kathy Hoopmann

When Ben and Andy discover an alien crashed landed in the backyard they are faced with a problem. They want to help Zeke repair his ship, but why does he ask for such strange things. Can they trust him?

Of Mice and Aliens is a book of mystery and fun. With Ben learning to cope with his newly diagnosed Asperger Syndrome, and Zeke trying to cope with life on Earth, things are not always as they seem.

'I would recommend this book to both parents and professionals. It is well written and sensitively portrays the difficulties faced by children and parents in living with Asperger's Syndrome. A list of support organisations and websites is given at the end of the story.'

— *Rostrum*

ISBN 1 84310 007 X

Lisa and the Lacemaker

An Asperger Adventure

Kathy Hoopmann

When Lisa discovers a derelict hut in her friend Ben's backyard, she delights in exploring the remnants of an era long gone. Imagine her surprise when Great Aunt Hannah moves into a nursing home nearby, and reveals that once she was a servant in those very rooms. The old lady draws Lisa into the art of lace making and through the criss-crossing of threads, Lisa is helped to understand her own Asperger Syndrome. But Great Aunt Hannah also has a secret and now it is up to Lisa to confront the mysterious Lacemaker and put the past to rest.

'Kathy Hoopmann has written a captivating adventure story but has also created a unique and accurate insight into the experiences and inner thoughts of a girl with Asperger's syndrome. Her central character faces challenges and develops coping strategies that we have only recently recognized. Children, parents and teachers will find the story both entertaining and an opportunity for education.'

— *Tony Attwood*

ISBN 1 84310 071 1